December Stillness

Also by Mary Downing Hahn

Following the Mystery Man
Tallahassee Higgins
Wait Till Helen Comes
The Jellyfish Season
Daphne's Book
The Time of the Witch
The Sara Summer

December Stillness

MARY DOWNING HAHN

Clarion Books
TICKNOR & FIELDS: A HOUGHTON MIFFLIN COMPANY
New York

Clarion Books
Ticknor & Fields, a Houghton Mifflin Company
Text copyright © 1988 by Mary Downing Hahn
Printed in the U.S.A.
P 10 9 8 7 6 5 4 3 2 1

Library of Congress Cataloging-in-Publication Data
Hahn, Mary Downing.
December stillness.
Summary: Thirteen-year-old Kelly tries to befriend
Mr. Weems, a disturbed homeless Vietnam War veteran
who spends his days in her suburban library, though
the man makes it clear he wants to be left alone.
[1. Veterans—Vietnam—Fiction.   2. Homeless
persons—Fiction]   I. Title.
PZ7.H1256De   1988   [Fic]   88-2572
ISBN 0-89919-758-2

Credits and Acknowledgments

Harper and Row: Quotations from "What's in the Sack?" from *Where the Sidewalk Ends* by Shel Silverstein. Copyright © 1974 by Evil Eye Music, Inc.

New Directions Publishing Company: Quotations from "Dulce et Decorum Est" and "Mental Cases" from *The Collected Poems of Wilfred Owen* by Wilfred Owen. Copyright © 1963 by Chatto and Windus, Ltd. Reprinted by permission of New Directions Pub. Corp.

Oxford University Press: Quotations from "The Return of the Greeks" from *Collected Poems* by Edwin Muir.

Viking Penguin Inc: Quotations from "December Stillness," "In the Pink," and "Repression of War Experience" from *Collected Poems* by Siegfried Sassoon.

For Kate

December Stillness

Chapter 1

WHEN I LEFT Mr. Poland's classroom, I saw Julie waiting for me by my locker, but she was too busy fussing with her hair to notice me walking toward her. She had a little mirror in one hand, her comb in the other, and she was staring at her reflection as if she expected it to speak to her.

"You, my queen, are the fairest of them all," I whispered in the sort of voice I imagined a magic mirror might have.

"Kelly, where have you been? It's ten past three." Julie tossed her hair once more, fluffing it with her hands.

"Mr. Poland wanted to talk to me about my current issues paper. He says I can't prove God is dead, I have to write about something more concrete."

"I knew he wouldn't approve a topic like that."

I shrugged. "He said he wanted us to pick controversial subjects, didn't he?"

"He meant stuff like abortion and child abuse and drunk driving, and you know it." Julie peeked at her reflection one more time, frowned, and thrust her mirror into her other pocket.

"Those are all so boring." I grabbed her comb and ran it through my hair. Why, I don't know. It's so short and curly it looks the same no matter what I do to it.

"So? That's what school's all about, doing boring things over and over." Julie snatched her comb and watched me turn the dial on my combination lock. "It prepares you for real life," she went on. "You know, getting a job and going to the same old place every day, cooking the same old meals every night, watching the same old shows on TV till you fall asleep."

"That may be the kind of life you're preparing for but not me." Yanking open my locker, I jumped back as an avalanche of books, papers, gym shoes, and umbrellas spewed out.

"When are you going to clean that locker out, McAllister?" Mr. Gleicher, the principal, appeared out of nowhere, one of his specialties. "It's a safety hazard."

He was making it sound like a joke, but I could tell he wasn't pleased. Picking up my scattered belongings, I said, "I know it looks like junk, but it's for a project I'm working on in art, sir. Miss Young wants us to make collages of our most cherished personal belongings, so I'm saving all my old homework papers for it."

Mr. Gleicher frowned which didn't surprise me. A senior might have been able to get away with a little impudence but not a lowly ninth grader, especially one he'd just called a super underachiever in our last interview. Nudging a wizened apple with the toe of his shiny loafer, he said, "What's this?"

I picked it up by the stem and watched it slowly revolve. It gave off a faint odor of decay. "My shrunken head," I cried. "I thought I'd lost it forever! My great-uncle Stanley, the famous explorer, brought it back from the Amazon. It's good luck, you know, like a rabbit's foot."

"Quit clowning and throw it in the trash, Mc-Allister." Mr. Gleicher scowled at me. "I'm going to inspect this locker tomorrow, and if it isn't in good shape, you can spend an hour in my office after school."

Turning his attention to Julie who hadn't opened her mouth once, he said, "And you, Sinclair. If you find this so entertaining, you'd better make sure your locker is clean too."

As he walked away, Julie stared at me. "Kelly, are you crazy?"

I crossed my eyes and danced around her, giggling. "Who, me? Me crazy? Me?"

She laughed then and helped me clean out my locker. That's why she's been my best friend since kindergarten — she puts up with every wacky thing I do and never gets mad at me, at least not for long.

"You have four umbrellas, Kelly." Julie held them up. "A red one, a blue one, a big black bumbershoot, and what looks like your dad's golf umbrella."

"You know me. I'm so into fashion I have to color coordinate everything, even my umbrellas."

I struck a pose with the golf umbrella. My dad had just missed it last week and was still searching for it. During his cross-examination, I'd claimed complete ignorance of its whereabouts, having conveniently forgotten I'd been forced to take it to school the last time it rained. What else was I supposed to do? Every other umbrella was already in my locker.

Julie, who of course is truly into fashion, ran a practiced eye over my paint-splattered sweatshirt, faded jeans, and worn-out running shoes. She watched me pull on my father's old army jacket and wrap a long striped scarf around my neck. "Right," she said. "Color coordination explains it all. "

As we left school, we cut across the soccer field to take a shortcut home through the woods. One of the nice things about a planned community like Adelphia, maybe the only nice thing, is the open space concept, the brainstorm of one of its developers. The builders had to set aside areas of woods and fields for tot lots and footpaths, and, as a result, you can walk for miles with nothing around you but trees and squirrels and an occasional groundhog or possum.

"So what are you going to write about, Kelly?" Julie turned up the collar of her jacket to shield her face from the cold.

"I don't know." I watched the November sun and wind play with Julie's hair, tossing it and making it shine red-gold.

"Didn't Mr. Poland give you any ideas?"

"Are you kidding? I don't think he'd recognize an idea if it fell out of the sky and hit him on the head." I opened the bumbershoot and held it aloft. "Maybe I'll just sail away on the wind like Mary Poppins and forget about Mr. Poland and current issues and every other boring thing." I did a little Julie Andrews dance step and started singing "Chimchimcheree."

"Oh, Kelly," Julie sighed. "I worry about you sometimes, I really do."

"Why?" I stared at her. "Don't you ever want to fly away from here, go someplace exciting, see the world? Do something besides worry about school?" Realizing I was flapping the umbrella, I collapsed it and tried to calm down. Lately I'd noticed Julie wasn't as enthusiastic about things as I was or at least not about the same things. She reserved her energy for boys, clothes, music, and school sports.

Julie shrugged. "Where would we go? We don't have jobs or money or anything. And besides," she added, "I like it here."

"How can you like the suburbs?" I waved the umbrella at the fields and woods, at the tot lot, at the line of town houses perched on the hill above us, row after row of wooden decks all sharing the same view. "Nothing ever happens here. It's all the same, day after day."

"There's worse places than Adelphia." Julie and I had reached her turnoff, and we lingered a minute, shivering as the wind buffeted us.

"Do you want to go to the library tonight?" Julie

asked. "My mom can drive if yours can pick us up."

"Sure."

"Courtney's going too. Is that okay?"

I shrugged. Courtney the brain wasn't one of my favorite people. Entirely too perfect to be anything but boring — straight *A*'s all her life, a pretty pink room full of swim team trophies, horse show ribbons, and citizenship awards, the kind of daughter all parents want. But which mine certainly didn't get. "I guess I can stand her for a couple of hours," I told Julie.

She tossed her hair again and rolled her eyes. "Oh, Kelly," she said, implying I was being too picky for words. "I'll see you at seven-thirty."

I watched her run up the path to Tiger Lily Court and then I headed for my house on Peter Pan Way, a few cul-de-sacs away. No matter how long I live in Adelphia, I'll never get used to the streets; every neighborhood is named after a famous author, and my parents, for reasons unknown to me, chose the J.M. Barrie area. Even the golf course, where my father spends most of his spare time, is called Pirate's Cove.

When I came out of the woods, I saw Keith Myers tossing a basketball through a net hanging over his garage door. Keith and I have been friends since I bit his leg in nursery school. As I remember the incident, he was using it to block the sliding board. Being a fairly aggressive three year old, I persuaded him to move his leg by sinking my teeth into it.

Now that we're in the ninth grade, Keith and I aren't as close as we used to be. Sometime in middle school, long after I'd stopped biting him, the other boys started teasing him about having a girl friend, so we stopped going everywhere together. Now he loves to embarrass me by calling me "Mad Dog McAllister" and asking to see my rabies tag. There are some things you would like to forget as you grow older.

I still like him though. Not the way Julie does, but just as another person, a good friend, somebody I used to have a lot of fun with.

When I was halfway across the street, I heard Keith yell, "Hey, Mad Dog, catch!"

The basketball flew at me and I caught it easily. I dribbled it away from him, keeping it close to the ground to take advantage of my height (barely five foot two) while he ran around me, lunging at the ball. After I shot a perfect basket, Keith snared the ball, taking advantage of *his* height.

"Not bad for a half pint." He smiled at me, revealing the braces that stood between him and total popularity. "Are you and Julie going to the library tonight?"

I knew he was trying hard to sound casual, so I said, "Maybe."

"Can I get a ride with you?"

"If we go."

"Come on, Mad Dog, you go every Thursday." He pretended to throw the ball at me, but I ignored him. I knew all his tricks by now.

I decided to tease him a little longer. "Julie's mother's driving. She might not have room for your big feet."

Keith looked at his basketball shoes. "They're not *that* big."

"Well, you know how Mrs. Sinclair is about boys."

"What do you mean?" Keith's voice cracked a little.

"Oh," I sighed, searching the autumn sky for a good lie, "She's already betrothed Julie to a Russian count and she doesn't want her getting interested in any tall, skinny basketball players."

"Get lost, Mad Dog!" Keith grabbed me around the waist and swung me around.

As I broke away, laughing, he yelled, "I'll be expecting Mrs. Sinclair to pick me up at seven-thirty, okay? I'll even help you with your algebra, Kelly."

From halfway up my sidewalk, I looked back. "You better. Palumbo's giving us a test Friday and I don't understand a single thing."

He waved before dribbling back to the net to shoot some more baskets, and I watched him for a few minutes before I went into the house. The afternoon sun backlit him, sending his long, thin shadow dancing ahead of him like an opponent as he bounced the ball in tight circles and jumped to send it curving toward the backboard.

As the ball whooshed through the net, I wondered if Keith were in love with Julie, and, just for a second, I wished I weren't so short and skinny. If I had long, red hair and a great figure instead of looking like somebody's kid brother, maybe I'd be the one Keith sat beside every time we rode to the library together.

Just then Keith glanced across the street and caught

me staring at him. "Hey, what's the matter, Mad Dog?" he shouted. "Did you lock yourself out again?"

I laughed and held up my key. Then I turned my back and fumbled with the door, glad Keith couldn't see how red my face was. He was my friend, my best buddy. Nobody could change that, not even Julie.

Chapter 2

"IS THAT YOU, Kelly?" Mom called when I dumped my books on the kitchen table.

"No, it's the mad killer of Adelphia, looking for a new victim," I shouted as I searched the refrigerator for something good to eat. "Are we all out of yogurt?"

"I ate the last one for lunch." Mom's voice floated down the steps against a background of old Simon and Garfunkel songs. "Look in the cupboard over the sink. I got some of those cookies you like while I was out jogging."

Grabbing a handful, I ran upstairs to Mom's studio. As I expected, I found her sitting at her drawing board painting a small picture of a unicorn with a wreath of holly around his neck. The afternoon sunlight streamed through the large windows and slanted across a wall of shelves filled with books and her collection of teddy bears, china dolls, puppets, and dragons of all sorts and sizes.

"Is that another Christmas card design?" I studied

the unicorn, carefully drawn in ink and tinted delicately with watercolor. For several years now, Mom has been selling fantasy cards to shops in Adelphia and Ellicott City. She started in a friend's bookstore with a little series of wizards, dragons, and unicorns, but now more and more shops are placing orders for her cards.

She smiled at me. Her nose had a little spot of red paint on its tip, and her fingers were ink-stained. "I've got three more to do before I take them to the printer next week. What do you think of the sketches?"

I looked at the drawings — a jovial wizard dressed like Santa Claus handing out presents to a group of animals, a castle with a wreath on its door, and a baby dragon puffing flames in a fireplace beneath a row of stockings. "They're cute, Mom," I said, "but don't you get a little tired of make-believe? You must be able to draw these creatures with your eyes closed by now."

Tipping back on her stool, Mom smiled at me. "How about fixing me a cup of tea, honey?"

I left her happily coloring the berries in the unicorn's wreath and trotted downstairs with my cat Gandalf at my heels.

As you can guess from her interest in make-believe, Mom named him after the wizard in Tolkien's books, Gandalf the Gray. Unfortunately, he hadn't grown up to be the lean hunter she thought he would be. Soft and lazy, our Gandalf preferred eating and dozing in sunny spots to going on quests. He was definitely a Hobbit, not a wizard, and Bilbo would have been a better name for him.

"No doubt you want something to eat too." I scooped him up and buried my face in his fur. "How about a cup of tea, my little Hobbit?"

He purred happily and leaped out of my arms. Sniffing his empty dish, he looked up at me hopefully.

I filled the kettle and set it on the stove, then dumped Meow Cat in Gandalf's dish, pushing him aside to keep his head out of the way. He's very greedy which is why he's a little chubby. Obese if you listen to my dad. But then he doesn't really like Gandalf — he just tolerates him the way he tolerates a lot of things. The current state of the world, for instance, the Stuart County education system, teenagers in general and me in particular.

While I fixed Mom's tea, I thought about her upstairs in her cozy hideaway, painting her dragons riding skateboards, her little girls hugging unicorns, her wizards floating aloft in hot-air balloons, her fairy-tale castles in the clouds.

Her drawings were good, better than a lot of pictures in children's books, but to me, illustration was second best. I wanted to be a real artist. I'd live by myself in a desert somewhere and paint all day, big canvases full of doom and gloom and truth. No wizards or dragons for me.

I stirred a spoonful of honey into Mom's tea and watched Gandalf sniff the floor around his dish. He was hoping he might somehow have overlooked a delicious morsel.

"I'll never give up," I told him as I picked him up

and peered deep into his big yellow eyes. "I'm going to be a real artist, Gandalf, you'll see."

To show his complete confidence in me, Gandalf began to purr and I hugged him. "Maybe you can come with me when I leave here," I said. "You can catch mice and sleep in the sun and be my best friend."

I tickled his chin, and then I took Mom her tea. Leaving her to work in peace, I went to my room and pulled out my own painting, a watercolor of a bare tree against a stormy sky. While I listened to my favorite Elvis Costello tape, I tried to highlight some of the branches, but the colors ran together and got muddy, and I ended up throwing it into the trash can.

*

By the time Dad came home, Mom and I had dinner ready, a tuna noodle casserole, a tossed salad, and a special loaf of pumpernickel from the German bakery.

"How was school today, Kelly?" Dad asked as we sat down to eat.

It was his standard question, so I gave my standard answer. "Okay."

"Did you tell your father what Miss Young said yesterday about your still life?" Mom prompted me.

Bending my head over my plate, I filled my mouth with noodles, hoping Dad would think I was too busy eating to answer. He and I have had a strained relationship ever since I started high school and failed to shape up academically. Art is all I care about, but he can't accept that. I don't know why. He doesn't mind Mom's artwork; in fact, he acts almost proud of her sometimes. But me — I can't do anything right. Clothes, hair, grades, attitude. The very sight of me seems to irritate him.

"She said it was nice," I said finally and glanced at Dad. He was spreading butter on a slice of bread, still wearing his suit jacket and tie, looking at me as if he were waiting for more words to drop from my lips.

"Oh, Kelly, don't be so modest." Mom turned to Dad. "Miss Young told Kelly she has a wonderful sense of composition and a great eye for color. She wants her to enter her still life in the Stuart County high school art show." Mom paused. "That's quite an honor for a ninth grader," she added when Dad didn't say anything.

"Very nice," Dad said, "but how about algebra?"

Algebra — that's the kind of thing he thinks is important. But what does he know? Lawyers have never been famous for their imaginations.

Since he was waiting for an answer, I said, "It's fine" and shoved some more lettuce into my mouth. I sensed the great attorney was getting ready to cross-examine me, and it was hard to swallow without choking. Why couldn't he ever be satisfied with me? Wasn't it good enough to be an artist, the best student Miss Young had ever had?

"Fine?" Dad stared at me. "What does that mean? A *D* instead of an *F* ?"

"Oh, Greg, for heaven's sake," Mom murmured.

Ignoring her, Dad went on presenting his case, "I want to see some real improvement on your report card this year, Kelly. You'll never get decent SAT scores if you don't do better in math. At the rate you're going, you'll be lucky to get into Stuart Community College."

"She wants to be an artist, not a mathematician, Greg," Mom interrupted.

"You don't seem to realize what a competitive world we live in, Martha." Dad leaned toward Mom, temporarily forgetting me. "Like it or not, Kelly needs some pushing if she's going to get into a good college."

"But I'm not going to college, Dad. I'm going to art school." I tried to sound reasonable, but my voice shook, and I felt like a little kid. "I don't need math. Or high SAT's."

"That's what you think." Dad turned toward me again, frowning. As he stabbed the air between us with hand gestures, I could feel myself slipping from a fourteen year old all the way down to a kindergartener.

"Check out the good schools, Kelly," he said. "Pratt, the Rhode Island School of Design — they want high scores just like any other college." He paused to take a swallow of wine, then added, "Art is fine, but you can't make a living painting. Save your creativity for a hobby and find a way to support yourself."

Before he could say anything else, I pushed my chair away from the table and reminded Mom about the library. "Mrs. Sinclair will be here any minute. Don't forget you're supposed to pick us up at nine."

Without looking at Dad, I ran up to my room to get my books. While I stuffed them into my backpack, I bit my lip, trying not to cry. Sometimes it seemed like Dad hated me. His tone of voice, the way he looked at me — why didn't I ever feel close to him anymore? If just once he would tell me he was proud of me, just once! Was that too much to expect from your father?

As I was buttoning my army jacket, I heard Mrs. Sinclair toot her horn out front. "Bye," I shouted as I ran out the door, glad to escape before the great attorney could make any more sarcastic observations.

∗

Keith and Courtney were already sitting in the back seat, so I had to crowd in next to the window. While the rest of them chattered about their current issues papers, I slouched in the corner, my nose pressed against the cold glass, and watched the dark streets slip past. Lights shone in the windows behind drawn drapes, gas lamps flickered in front yards, joggers and dog walkers trotted along the sidewalks.

Everybody was happy but me. Keith and Julie and Courtney, Mrs. Sinclair, even the joggers. I saw a little girl walking beside her father, holding his hand, laughing at something he said, and I felt like crying. Once I was a kid like that, glad to be with my dad, but now everything was different. I wasn't happy with Dad or anybody else.

By the time we got to the library I was really depressed. Nobody had said a word to me. They'd been too busy talking about how great the Owen Mills basketball team was to notice how quiet I was. My friends, I thought, three people I'd known almost all my life, and I was drifting away from them, feeling more and more set apart. What did I care about basketball? And school spirit? It seemed so trivial.

Mrs. Sinclair pulled into the library's crowded parking lot behind several other cars disgorging teenagers. "Your mother's picking everybody up?" she asked me.

I nodded, anxious to escape the car and the overwhelming scent of Mrs. Sinclair's perfume.

"You stay at the library, Julie," Mrs. Sinclair added before she drove away. "No running across the street to the mall. I'm planning to do some shopping, and I don't want to catch you stuffing your face at the Eatery."

"Don't worry, Mom, I've got tons of research to do for Mr. Poland."

As we walked away, Julie muttered, "Of all the luck. I was planning on a little snack break around eight."

When we all laughed, the clerks at the library checkout counter looked up and frowned. I knew they were thinking, "Oh, no, not that bunch. There goes our peace and quiet."

"Shush, you guys," Courtney muttered. "Do you want us to get kicked out or something?"

Unlike the rest of us, Courtney takes school and libraries very seriously. In fact, she's already worried about her SAT's and whether she'll get into a good college. Naturally she's the only one of my friends who's earned the great attorney's seal of approval.

We found a table upstairs in the reference room. Julie and Keith sat next to each other and started talking about their current issues reports. Keith was doing his on animal rights, something he's been interested in all his life, and Julie was doing hers on euthanasia.

While they giggled about something, Courtney draped her parka over a chair and headed for the *Readers' Guide to Periodical Literature;* like a good student, she was looking up magazine articles to use for her report on capital punishment.

"Hey, I thought you were going to help me with algebra." I kicked Keith under the table.

"Some other time, Mad Dog," Keith said. "I want to get started on this report tonight."

"You better pick a topic, Kelly," Julie said. "It's due the week after Thanksgiving, and it's seventy percent of this quarter's grade."

"I know that." I scowled at Julie. Did she have to nag me too?

"I thought you were proving God is dead or something," Keith said.

"Mr. Poland claims it's inappropriate." I slumped down in my chair and gazed around the reference room. Most of the tables were occupied by kids, some from Owen Mills High School, some from All View, some from Arundel. Most of them were working, but a few of them were laughing and talking. Every time they got too loud, the librarian at the information desk would give them a warning look. Sometimes she even got up and told them to be quiet.

One table, though, she always avoided. Everybody did. It was the bagman's table. Whenever I came to the library, he was sitting there, a short, skinny guy with a wild tangle of brown hair and a bushy beard, wearing old army clothes so grimy the olive green had turned gray. At his side were two black plastic bags, the kind you see lined up at the curb on garbage collection day. They were bulging with stuff, and he never left them, not even to go to the men's room.

Sometimes I'd see him, bent almost double by the weight of his bags, staggering along the side of the road. He reminded me of some weird mythic figure like the Wandering Jew, cursed forever to wander the earth without rest, bearing his terrible burden.

In Baltimore and Washington you wouldn't even notice the bagman, but he really stood out in Adelphia. There weren't any homeless people here. Everybody had a place to call home and enough money for food. The bagman was truly one of a kind.

Glancing at him, I noticed he was reading what looked like a travel book, and I wondered if the librarians fumigated everything he handled. The air around him smelled awful, but the odor came mainly from his bags, I thought. God knows what he had in them. Some of the boys swore it was dead cats he picked up on the side of the road or several hundred pounds of well-aged Limburger cheese. But I guessed it was probably dirty clothes and ratty old blankets and raggedy tennis shoes — everything he owned, filthy and damp and full of mildew.

While I was staring at him, he looked up, made a telescope with his hands, and peered around the reference room. Catching my eye, he bent his head quickly over his book, as if he were embarrassed.

I turned to Julie and Keith, thinking they'd enjoy the bagman's weird antics, but Julie was whispering in Keith's ear and he was laughing. They were sitting as close to each other as they could, and it was obvious they had forgotten all about me. I wanted to kick Keith again, really hard this time, but I just bit my lip and doodled a likeness of the bagman on a piece of notebook paper, making him look wilder and hairier and more grotesque than he really was.

The bagman coughed and I looked at him again. He was scratching his head with one hand and his shoulder with the other. Two girls were watching him and giggling, and a couple of adults were scowling as if they'd never seen a more repulsive sight.

That's when my great idea came to me. I leaned across the table and poked Keith's hand with my pen. "I just thought of a topic for my report," I said, keeping my face straight so they'd think I was serious.

"Well, it's about time, Mad Dog," Keith said. "What's the subject — rabies?"

"Cool it, you guys." I shook my bangs out of my eyes and glared at Julie to make her quit giggling. "I'm going to write about the homeless."

"Oh, that's a good idea," Julie said. "For your interview, you could call that guy in Washington, you know the one who runs the creative violence shelters."

"Creative Non-Violence, you airhead." Keith laughed and cracked Julie on the head with his pencil.

"Whatever," Julie said. "He'd be pretty interesting, I bet. He's even been on TV, Kelly. Remember? They made a movie of his life, starring that actor Martin Sheen."

"I don't need to talk to Mitch Snyder," I said, trying not to laugh, "or go to Washington. I can start right here in Adelphia." I pointed my pen at the bagman who was now nodding off, his head almost touching his book. "I'm interviewing *him*."

Chapter 3

JULIE AND KEITH stared at me as if I'd lost my mind. I'd wanted their attention, and now I definitely had it.

"Are you serious?" Keith asked as Julie said, "Oh, Kelly, you wouldn't!"

"What wouldn't Kelly do?" Courtney paused by the table. She was on her way to the information desk with a handful of periodical request forms.

"She wants to interview *him* for her current issues report." Julie pointed none too subtly at the bagman who was sound asleep now with his head on the book.

Courtney dropped down into the chair next to me. "Even you wouldn't do that," she whispered. "He's filthy and gross and probably crazy too. You'd get lice just going near him."

"We're supposed to have a primary source, remember?" I asked her. I hadn't enjoyed myself so much for a long time — Mad Dog McAllister, the craziest girl in Adelphia, that was me all right. Struggling to keep from laughing, I leaned toward them, loving every minute of their shocked attention. "That was one of the problems with my God paper," I reminded Courtney, "I didn't have anyone to interview."

"So call social services or something," Courtney said in her mature, I'm-giving-you-good-advice voice. "That's what everybody's doing. I'm certainly not going to talk to a criminal on death row about capital punishment."

"Think how much better your paper would be, though, if you did talk to somebody about to be executed," I said. "Mr. Poland would be so impressed, he'd give you an $A+$ for sure."

"I'll get an $A+$ no matter what I do," Courtney said with her usual modesty. She leaned toward me. "And do you know why? Because I don't goof off or get weird ideas."

I glanced at Keith and rolled my eyes. "There's nothing weird about interviewing a homeless person," I said.

"Oh, come on, Kelly," Julie said, "You don't have the nerve to go over there and ask him anything."

"You want to bet?" I stood up and looked down at the three of them.

"I bet you a Reese's Pieces sundae at Friendly's, Mad Dog," Keith said, going right for my Achilles' heel. If there's one thing I can't resist it's ice cream.

"Watch me." As I picked up my notebook and my pen, Keith grabbed my arm.

"Ask him what's in the bags," he whispered.

"Yes," Julie agreed. "I'd give anything to know. I mean, he lugs them everywhere. It must be something incredible."

"Yuck." Courtney wrinkled her nose. "Whatever it is, I don't want to know. It smells like garbage or something even more gross."

I shoved my chair back and started walking across the room. Behind me, I heard Keith say, "She won't do it."

"I can't believe this." Courtney sounded kind of hysterical. "She's walking right up to him."

When I glanced at them over my shoulder, I saw Julie collapse into one of her giggling fits. Courtney had a book in front of her face, and Keith was tipped back in his chair shaking his head and grinning. By this time, I was standing by the bagman's table, looking down at his matted hair, and trying not to breathe too deeply. This close, the stench was really nauseating.

Either the bagman hadn't actually been asleep or he was very alert, because his head snapped up and he looked at me. Not at my face, just at my sweater. Then he bent over his book and began reading, his finger tracing each line of print. From here, I could see it was a book of war photographs. I don't know which war. Combat photos all look the same to me. Mud and bodies and tanks.

"Excuse me, sir," I said with exaggerated politeness.

I was hoping I wouldn't laugh, not with everybody in the whole reference room watching me, including Mrs. Martin, the librarian.

The bagman ignored me, so I sat down across from him, breathing through my mouth to avoid being overwhelmed. "I wondered if I could ask you some questions," I continued, trying to sound like a reporter on Live Action News.

He didn't look up from a hideous picture of a heap of dead bodies, but he shook his head very slowly, back and forth.

Behind me I could hear Julie snorting through her nose like an elephant trumpeting. Keith was laughing too and so were a lot of other kids. Somebody said, "Who *is* that girl?"

"I'm interviewing homeless people, sir," I told the bagman, "and I'd really appreciate your giving me a few minutes of your time."

Again he shook his head, more vigorously this time, but he still didn't look at me. The laughter was getting louder, so I said, "Can you tell me what you've got in those bags?" Unable to control myself any longer, I started laughing too.

He continued shaking his head and made little motions with his hands as if he were pushing me away. Julie snorted again, and a guy at the next table said, "Girl, you're something else." I was beginning to feel like a star. In fact, I almost expected to hear applause.

Before I could ask any more questions, though, I felt someone's hand touch my shoulder. I looked up and there was Mrs. Martin. She was not laughing, and she did not look amused.

"May I speak to you?" she asked in a voice cold enough to freeze Niagara Falls.

As I followed her back to the information desk, I noticed that Julie was laughing, Keith was running a finger across his throat like a knife, and Courtney was still hiding behind her book. Practically everybody else was watching me, though.

"Why were you bothering Mr. Weems?" Mrs. Martin wanted to know.

"I wasn't bothering him." Getting my laughter under control, I slouched on one hip and tried to look cool. "I'm doing a report on the homeless," I said, "and we have to have one primary source. You know, somebody to interview. I just wanted to ask him a few questions, that's all." I shifted my weight to my other hip and tossed my hair out of my eyes, hoping Mrs. Martin couldn't hear my heart going *thump thump* like a scared rabbit.

"I know Mr. Weems is a little different from most library patrons," Mrs. Martin said in a low voice, "but he never disturbs anyone, and he has a right to expect the same treatment from others. It was very obvious he didn't want to answer your questions."

I shrugged, aware of my audience. "I guess I'll just have to try some other time," I said.

She looked at me sharply. "If I see you bothering him again, I'll have to ask you to leave the library."

"So much for freedom of speech," I said loudly and

walked back to my table, feeling lots of eyes, including Mrs. Martin's, track me across the room.

"Oh, Kelly," Julie snorted, "I can't believe you did that." Her face was red from laughing and her eyes had tears in them.

"Me either." Keith looked sad. "Now I have to buy you a Reese's Pieces, Mad Dog."

Courtney put down her book and frowned at me. "I don't see anything funny about it," she said. "We could've gotten kicked out of here."

"If only I could be as mature as you, Courtney," I said, trying to sound as sarcastic as my dad.

Ignoring me, she turned her attention to a magazine article called "Life on Death Row — How does it feel to know when you're going to die?"

"I think the librarian's in love with Mr. Weems," I told Julie. That set her off, and we laughed till Mrs. Martin herself marched up to our table.

"If I have to tell you one more time to be quiet, you're out for the night," she said. "You're disturbing everybody."

"Me?" I stared at her. "I wasn't the only one laughing."

"I know an instigator when I see one."

As Mrs. Martin walked back to her desk, Courtney glared at me. "Oh, Kelly," she whispered, "why don't you grow up?"

By now I was getting tired of the reference room, but I knew I was stuck there for another forty-five minutes. Sighing loudly, I pulled my world literature book out of my backpack and opened it to the *Iliad,* our current reading assignment. I was in Honors English, my one serious *A* course — since art didn't count as far as my dad was concerned — and Mr. Hardy was my favorite teacher.

Even though I hated the blood-and-gore battle scenes, I was impressed by the things Mr. Hardy said about the poem. If you thought about it, he claimed, the *Iliad* was really an antiwar poem. For one thing, the reason for fighting was totally irrational. What did the ordinary soldier care about Helen? Let Paris keep her, they probably thought. Mr. Hardy also said Achilles was proud, cruel, and selfish. When he killed Hector, his moral superior in every way, he struck a blow against civilization.

Achilles wasn't the hero of the *Iliad,* Mr. Hardy said. Hector was. His death made the poem a tragedy, not just for one man but for an entire people.

I was reading the scene where Hector says good-bye to his wife and baby son. The little boy shrinks away from the plume on Hector's helmet. He doesn't recognize his father, so Hector takes off the helmet. It's really a sad scene, mainly because you know Hector is going to die and Troy is going to be destroyed and Greek soldiers are going to kill the little boy and take his mother into slavery.

Whatever the *Iliad* was — tragedy, antiwar poem, epic — I just wasn't in the mood to read any more of it. Closing my book, I glanced across the room just in time to see Mr. Weems peek at me through his telescope hands. When he realized I was looking at him, he dropped his hands and bent his head over his book again. Nobody else noticed, but it made me feel weird, and I wondered how long he'd been watching me.

*

Mom showed up promptly at nine and drove us home, dropping Courtney off without noticing she and I weren't speaking. Julie was next, and Keith told Mom he'd walk back from her house. As we pulled away, I saw him kiss Julie.

"Well, is that a little romance?" Mom asked.

"I guess so." I fiddled with the radio dial, found a great U2 song, and turned it up loud so Mom wouldn't say any more about Keith and Julie. It bothered me to think about them kissing, and I didn't want to talk about it.

When we got home, I tried to sneak upstairs without encountering Dad, but he spotted me slouching past his den. Looking up from a pile of paperwork, he asked me if I'd accomplished anything at the library.

"I got a lot of reading done," I said uneasily.

"You could have done that here at home." Dad frowned at me.

"I mean magazines and stuff. I was doing research for a report." I thought of Courtney and wondered what it would be like to tell your parents the truth about studying.

"What report is this?"

"Oh, just something on current issues for Mr. Poland." I edged away down the hall, toward the steps and the safety of my room.

"Current issues?" Dad got up and followed me. "What's your topic?" He actually sounded interested.

"Homeless people," I mumbled. Even though I hadn't been at all serious in the library, I couldn't think of anything else to tell Dad. Actually it seemed as good as anything to write a stupid paper on.

"Do a good job with it, Kelly," Dad said. "As I told you at dinner, you really have to improve your grades."

I nodded, not wanting him to get started again on my scholastic achievement.

"Oh, don't look at me like that." Dad reached out and touseled my hair, trying to make it all sound like a joke. "You're too smart to waste your mind — can't you see that?"

*

Safe in my room at last, I snuggled under my quilt, trying to make a nice warm little nest for myself. As I listened to the wind prowling around the corners of the house, I thought of Mr. Weems. Somewhere outside in the cold night, he was probably staggering along a roadside. I pictured the headlights of passing cars illuminating his face and bags for a few seconds, then dropping him back into darkness, a bogyman from a nightmare, wild-eyed and alone.

Over his head, the stars glittered and the moon slid in and out of the clouds, but he didn't look up. He walked bent over, the bags weighing him down. All he saw was the road stretching before him. All he felt was the icy wind tugging at his clothes.

I burrowed deeper under my covers and tried to shut out the sound of the wind. I didn't want to think about Mr. Weems out there in the night, cold and alone, not while I was safe and warm in bed.

But I couldn't make his face go away. I kept seeing the fear in his eyes and the little gestures he'd made to ward me off. Here in the dark, all by myself, the memory of what I'd said to him made me squirm. To make my friends laugh, I'd made a fool of Mr. Weems. And of myself, too.

Now that it was too late, I really wanted to talk to him, to find out where he went at night, how he got his meals, how he lived. But he'd never trust me now. Not after I'd acted so stupid.

Before I fell asleep, I told myself I'd apologize to Mr. Weems. Somehow I'd convince him I wasn't the terrible person he thought I was. I'd help him, I'd be his friend. If he'd let me.

Chapter 4

THE NEXT DAY, Mr. Poland cornered me before class. "Have you picked a topic for your paper yet, McAllister?"

I nodded, hoping to slide past him and into the classroom, but he laid a hand on my arm.

"Do you realize you're right on the border between pass and fail this quarter?" he asked. "If you expect a *C* from me, you'd better turn in a good paper."

Instead of answering, I shrugged and tried again to slip past him and into the classroom.

"What does it take to wake you up, McAllister?" Mr. Poland blocked the doorway and frowned at me. "I know you have a mind. When are you going to use it?"

Before I could think of an answer, two girls in my class ran up to Mr. Poland and started pestering him about the test he was going to give us.

"Will it have that stuff about Iran and Iraq on it?" Cindy wanted to know.

"Please say no, please," Jennifer giggled. "We

weren't here the day you talked about it, remember? We were at pompom practice, so we shouldn't have to know about it, right?"

Leaving Mr. Poland to deal with them, I went to my seat and opened my notebook. I wanted to finish the drawing of Miss Kennedy I'd started in French; she had an interesting face, and I thought I'd gotten a good likeness, especially the cheekbones, high and slanted, which gave her a slightly exotic look. What difference did Iran and Iraq make to me? I hadn't studied, so I was probably going to fail the test no matter what was on it.

*

After school, Julie had a dental appointment, so I decided to walk to the library. If Mr. Weems was there, I'd try talking to him again. Seriously this time.

When I went up to the reference room, I saw Mr. Weems sitting in his usual place, barricaded by a pile of books and his bags. Unfortunately for me, Mrs. Martin was on duty at the information desk again. She glanced up from a file of index cards, saw me, and frowned. Knowing it was useless to approach Mr. Weems with Mrs. Martin watching me, I ran back downstairs to the children's room.

You might think a fourteen year old has no business in the little kids' section of the library, but it's been my favorite place since Mom started bringing me there for story programs when I was three. It's a big sunny room, full of hanging plants and stuffed animals and picture books, but the main reason I go is to see Mrs.

Hunter, the children's librarian. Besides Mom, she and Mr. Hardy are almost the only adults I can talk to.

"Hi, Kelly." Mrs. Hunter looked up from the book she was reading and smiled at me. "What wind blew you this way?"

"A cold one." I dropped down into the chair beside her desk and contemplated the book in front of her. "Is that good?"

She nodded. "It's a great fantasy," she said. "Your mom would love it."

I nodded in agreement when she showed me the cover. Dragons and wizards, castles and unicorns. Definitely Mom's kind of book.

"So how's school?" Mrs. Hunter asked.

"Even crummier than usual." I slid down in the chair and contemplated my feet. "I have to do a big paper for my global perspectives class, and, if I don't get a good grade, I'll fail this quarter."

"What's your topic?"

"Well, first I wanted to prove God was dead, but Mr. Poland wouldn't let me, so I decided last night I'd write about the homeless. Just for a joke, I tried to interview that bagman who comes in here all the time, but I goofed it all up acting dumb and showing off. Mrs. Martin told me to leave him alone, so I'll probably never get another chance to talk to him." Just telling Mrs. Hunter about it made my face heat up with embarrassment.

"I've never seen Mr. Weems speak to anyone, Kelly," Mrs. Hunter said thoughtfully. "He comes in every morning and stays till we close, reading books about Vietnam. Somebody told me he's a veteran."

"Is that why he's so weird?" I'd heard about what Vietnam did to people. In fact, Mr. Hardy had been talking about it just the other day, drawing a few parallels between Vietnam and the Trojan War. Like us, he said, the Greeks were fighting in a foreign land for an unpopular cause, dying to satisfy their leaders' pride. Then he read us something an English poet, Edwin Muir, had written about the soldiers returning from Troy, "Sleepwandering from the war." Just like the Vietnam veterans, no honor, no glory, just scars, rags and tatters. "All the world was strange," he read, "After ten years of Troy."

"It could explain his behavior," Mrs. Hunter said. "Some veterans never got over the war. They couldn't fit back into normal life when they came home."

"My dad was in Vietnam, but he doesn't have any problems." I thought of my father raking in thousands of dollars every year in corporate law. No rags and tatters for him. No scars either.

"This is his army jacket." I pointed to Dad's name sewed on the front. "I found it in a box of old stuff he was throwing out. It really bugs him when I wear it. Especially since I did this to it." I turned around and showed her the big peace sign I'd painted on the back.

"Have you ever asked your father about the war?" Mrs. Hunter asked.

"Are you kidding? He never talks about it, never. He gets mad if you even mention it."

"It might bother him more than you realize, Kelly."

I shook my head. "You don't know my dad. All he cares about is money." I was telling the truth. The only time I ever heard my father complain about the government was in April when he was figuring out his taxes. Wars, nuclear weapons, pollution, acid rain, starvation in Africa — stuff like that meant nothing to him.

While Mrs. Hunter mulled this over, a mother with a couple of children in tow approached the desk and asked her if she had any short, easy-to-read biographies. "Janie is supposed to do a book report on a famous person," the mother explained as Janie and her little brother exchanged pokes, "but she doesn't like to read. Can you recommend something short that might interest her?"

I watched Mrs. Hunter lead them away, telling the little girl about Helen Keller. Then I wandered over to the poetry section to look for one of my old favorites, *Where the Sidewalk Ends* by Shel Silverstein. Finding a well-read copy on the shelf, I sat down on a cushion under a sunny window and turned to Cynthia Sylvia Stout and her disastrous refusal to take the garbage out. Flipping back and forth, pausing to laugh at more of my favorites, I came to a poem I'd forgotten about.

I stared at the illustration Silverstein had drawn to go with it, a sad man bent double by the weight of an enormous sack. Then I read the poem. It was about a man like Mr. Weems who was pestered by people who wanted to know what was in his sack. "Is it love letters or downy goosefeathers?" they asked, "Or maybe the world's most enormous balloon?"

They never asked, "Hey, when's your birthday?" or wanted to know where he'd been or how long he'd be staying or when he'd be back. They never said, "'How do?' or 'What's new?' or 'Hey, why are you blue?'"

It was the saddest poem I'd ever read, the only one in the book that couldn't make me laugh. How awful Mr. Weems must feel — people staring at him, laughing at him, making fun of his bags and never caring how he felt. Remembering the way I'd pranced up to his table last night, I felt hot and prickly all over. How could I have been so awful?

Putting the book back on the shelf, I waved to Mrs. Hunter who was still looking for the perfect biography and went upstairs to the reference room. This time, I saw Miss McCarthy sitting at the information desk. As usual, she was too absorbed in the thriller she was reading to notice anything.

Without actually looking at Mr. Weems, I pulled a book about Vietnam off the shelf and, forcing myself to overlook the rancid smell surrounding him, I sat down at his table. While I read, I glanced at him from time to time. I knew he was aware of me. Every now and then, he made his telescope and peered at me, but he didn't say anything.

What would happen, I wondered, if I showed him Silverstein's poem or just asked him, "Hey, when is your birthday? Where have you been? How long will you be staying? Where are you going? When will you be back?" Would he just flutter his hands again to ward me off? Or would he tell me?

Without anybody to egg me on, though, I was too much of a coward to speak to him. Instead, I turned the pages of the book, gazing at one depressing picture after another. How could soldiers, men like my dad, kill and burn and destroy? No wonder Mr. Weems was so messed up. If I'd been a man in the sixties, I'd have burned my draft card and gone to Canada before I'd have gotten involved in the kind of things I saw in the photographs.

I was getting so depressed thinking about war and killing and stuff like that, I decided to leave without saying anything to Mr. Weems. I just couldn't deal with all the terrible things he must have seen and done.

As I gathered up my belongings, though, I stole a look at him. His head was bent over a Vietnam combat photograph, and I could see the white skin on the back of his neck. "Where are you going?" I whispered, quoting Shel Silverstein, "and when will you be back?"

If he heard me, he paid no attention. In fact, I wasn't even sure he was awake. Quietly I left him sitting there, his secrets safe from me and Mrs. Martin and everyone else.

Chapter 5

BY THE TIME I got home, it was almost dark. Dad's car was parked in the driveway, and I could see him and Mom in the kitchen window. She was standing at the stove, her long hair hiding her face, and he was talking to her, smiling and gesturing.

For a few minutes, I stood on the lawn watching them as if they were performers in a play. What was it Shakespeare said? Something about strutting and fretting your hour on the stage. That was Dad all right. Strutting and fretting about everything. But not Mom. She was so quiet. How did she put up with his performances?

From talking to my friends, I know almost everybody wonders about their parents. Why they got married, why they stay together, stuff like that. Most of the time, parents hardly talk to each other, and they never do anything interesting or exciting. You get the feeling they're just occupying a house together, strangers living in the same hotel exchanging pleasantries like, "Please pass the pepper."

My parents are no exception. As far as I can see, what matters to Dad is his career, golf, and jogging. What matters to Mom is her artwork. They eat meals together, share the same bed, and go out every now and then. And that's it.

I often wonder where I fit into the scheme of things. Am I the glue holding them together? Or the wedge driving them apart? After all, I seem to be at the center of most of their disagreements with Mom defending me and Dad criticizing me.

When I was a little kid wearing Oshkosh overalls, looking just like Dad thought a little kid should look, he played with me. I actually have a picture tacked to my bulletin board to prove it. He's tossing me up in the air and we're both laughing. Like all color photos, the sky is blue and the sun is shining and we look like we're having a wonderful time.

Later he drove me to swim meets and soccer games and cheered for me even when I didn't do very well. But then I got older, and I didn't want to be on the swim team and I didn't want to play soccer and I grew out of my Oshkoshes. I wasn't cute any more. And I didn't like school and everything changed somehow.

It's been four years since I kicked a ball past a goalie, but Dad still hasn't adjusted. He says things like, "I saw Courtney's picture in the *Flier* yesterday, making a point for the Owen Mills soccer team. Remember when you two played together in elementary school?" I know he's wondering why it's Courtney who's a superstar instead of me.

Well, I couldn't stand there on the lawn all night trying to figure it out. I was getting too cold and hungry, so I ran up the walk and opened the front door. "I'm home," I yelled.

"It's about time." Dad frowned at me as I dumped my backpack on the kitchen floor and tossed my jacket over a chair. "We have a closet, Kelly," he said pointedly.

"Where have you been?" Mom gave me a kiss. "Your nose is cold," she added.

"At the library."

"Two days in a row?" Dad feigned amazement. "Is this the beginning of an intellectual trend?"

Ignoring his sarcasm, I said, "I was doing some research." Without looking at him, I took the plate of spaghetti Mom handed me and carried it into the dining room.

When we were all seated, Dad turned to me. "Well, Kelly," he said, "how is the current issues paper coming?"

"Okay." I looked away from Dad, down at the floor. Gandalf was sitting by my feet, looking soulfully into my eyes, hoping I was about to drop a meatball.

"Your father tells me your topic is the homeless," Mom said.

"I want to interview this bagman," I told Mom. "He's at the library every day, but he won't talk to me.

He just sits at a table reading books about Vietnam. Mrs. Hunter thinks he's a veteran. I guess that's what's wrong with him."

"Does he carry a couple of plastic garbage bags?" Dad asked. "Just bulging with stuff?"

I nodded. "He never puts them down; he takes them everywhere."

"I told you about him, Martha," Dad said. "I see him every morning, walking along the side of the road. I always wondered where he was going."

"His name is Mr. Weems," I said, "and he's going to the library."

"But where does he live?" Mom looked concerned. "It's so cold at night."

"Don't waste your time worrying about him," Dad muttered. "He doesn't have to live that way, not with all the handouts he can get from Uncle Sam."

"But, Greg," Mom said, "he may be too mentally disturbed to know where to go for help."

As Dad took a sip of wine, a gust of wind shook the glass in the sliding glass doors and sent a swirl of dead leaves scuttling across the deck outside the dining room.

"Mr. Hardy says lots of guys were really messed up in Vietnam," I said.

"Oh, no," Dad sighed. "Not Mr. Hardy, the world's leading expert on the Vietnam War. Please, no quotes from him tonight."

"You were in Vietnam." I leaned toward Dad, trying to force him to look at me. "You saw what happened."

"And look at me. Do you see me walking around carrying my belongings in a garbage bag, dressed in rags, no job, no home?" His voice rose a little.

"Of course not. Everybody knows you're the great attorney." I picked up my empty plate and glass and walked out to the kitchen. I could be sarcastic too, I thought, as I went upstairs to my room, ignoring Mom's plea to come back for dessert.

*

When I woke up on Saturday morning, I found Gandalf sleeping on my chest, all twenty-five pounds of him. The wind was blowing harder than ever, a real November gale, and I could feel cold air creeping in under the edges of my blankets.

"Well, Gandalf, excuse me." Shoving him aside, I got up and rummaged in the clothes littering the floor, looking for something warm. I found my favorite rag wool sweater under the bed. It's the kind L.L.Bean sells for twenty dollars, but I only paid fifty cents for it at Goodwill. Sure it has holes in both elbows and it's kind of baggy and all, but that's the way I like my clothes. Ten sizes too big and already broken in.

When I opened the refrigerator, Dad looked up from his cup of coffee. "You're up early," he said.

"I was freezing to death," I said. Finding the raisin bread, I grabbed the margarine and the apricot jam and started fixing breakfast.

As I sat down, Dad frowned. "Is that all you're eating? Raisin bread and jam?"

"It's good." I bit into the bread and felt jam squish

out of the corners of my mouth. I licked it off, knowing I was grossing him out.

Dad sighed and watched me take another bite. "That sweater looks awful," he said. "It's got holes in the elbows, it's too big, and it's dirty. Are you trying to look like a bag person?"

"Maybe." I licked jam from my fingers and sipped my coffee.

Dad walked to the sink and rinsed his cup before putting it in the dishwasher. "Clean up after you finish," he said as he left the kitchen.

"Where's Mom?" I called after him.

"In dragon land. Where else?" Then he went into his den, and I knew he was going to settle down for a long round with his computer.

After I'd gulped the rest of my breakfast, I ran upstairs to see Mom. As Dad said, she was sitting at her drawing table, carefully inking in a dragon pulling Santa's sleigh. The cold November sun shone down through the skylight, bringing out the silver in her brown hair.

I flopped into an old armchair and Gandalf jumped into my lap, purring as he made himself comfortable. "Do you think Dad's right about Mr. Weems?"

"What do you mean?" Mom asked.

"That he's just a bum using Vietnam as an excuse."

"Oh, Kelly, you know how your father is." Mom sighed and continued shading the dragon with tiny crosshatched pen strokes. "He's so uptight about the war."

"Hasn't he ever talked to you about it?"

"No." She bent her head over the dragon, concentrating on the tiny scales in his tail.

"But didn't you meet him at one of those antiwar demonstrations?"

"Well, yes, but I was the one protesting, not him. He was just passing by actually, and he rescued me from a cop who was threatening to arrest me." Mom smiled and shook her head; in her memory, she was seeing a man I'd never known, a man I couldn't even imagine.

Slumping down in the chair, I ruffled Gandalf's thick gray fur. "You must have asked him about the war, though," I finally said.

She nodded. "I thought he'd want to talk about it, but he clammed up every time I mentioned it."

I watched her touch the dragon's scales lightly with a pale mauve wash. "Was he for the war? Or against it?"

She shook her head. "He didn't think demonstrations did any good." She smiled, seeing that stranger again. "You should have seen Greg then. Long hair, beard, old army clothes and blue jeans, just like everybody else. My parents almost died the first time they met him."

"Dad was a *hippie*?" I snorted so loud Gandalf gave me a dirty look. "Come on, Mom. The great attorney living in a crash pad?"

"Well, it wasn't exactly a crash pad. He and a couple of other vets rented an apartment near the university, a real pigpen. Socks drying on the radiators, sink full of dirty dishes, unmade beds, plants on every window sill, Grateful Dead posters curling off the walls." She laughed. "The roaches were as big as rats, I swear they were."

I bent my head over Gandalf and tried to visualize Dad living in a pigpen, wearing clothes with holes in them, listening to the Grateful Dead. But all I could see was the man I'd always known, the one in the three-piece suit nagging me to clean my room, change my clothes, comb my hair, the one who kept the car radio tuned to elevator music and had his hair styled, the one who once told me rock music was destroying my brain.

"So when did the big change take place?" I asked Mom, giving up the struggle to imagine Dad as a hippie.

"Oh, he settled down after he finished law school. Cut his hair, shaved off his beard, bought a suit." She sighed. "By the time you were born, he was quite respectable."

"Weren't you disappointed?" I was wondering how I'd feel if Keith turned out to be just like Dad. All his life, he'd cared about animals; he wanted to save the whales and keep hunters from killing baby seals. He was the only person I knew who gave money to Greenpeace and refused to wear leather shoes and never ate meat, not even fish. Suppose he decided to become a lawyer specializing in corporate law? He wouldn't be Keith anymore. And I'd be really disillusioned.

"I changed too." Mom gave me a long look that suggested a lot of things she wasn't willing to put into words. Dipping her brush into a wash of blue, she bent over her picture. "If you don't mind, honey, I have work to do."

"It looks like play to me." I frowned at her as I walked past her drawing table, but she didn't look up from her little dragon.

Well, I wasn't going to change, I told myself as I went downstairs. I'd rather be a bum like Mr. Weems than give up my dreams. At least he was free to go wherever he wanted. He wasn't tied to a drawing table or a computer keyboard. He was out in the world. Cold sometimes. Maybe hungry. But free. Like Thoreau, he marched to a different drummer — what was wrong with that?

Chapter 6

WHILE I WAS pouring Cat Meow in Gandalf's dish, I had a great idea. Maybe if I fixed lunch for Mr. Weems, he'd realize I cared about him.

Quickly I made three sandwiches, heaping slabs of cheese and leftover beef on lettuce and topping them off with sliced tomatoes and gobs of Dad's best mustard. When I was satisfied the mall's finest deli couldn't have made better sandwiches, I wrapped them and put them in a paper bag along with a juicy navel orange, a banana, and two apples. Then I filled my old Wonder Woman thermos with coffee from Dad's pot and tossed a can of V–8 juice in the bag along with everything else.

As I stood at the closet door pulling on my army jacket, I noticed Dad's rag wool mittens on the shelf. He wore them on the rare occasions when he and Mom went cross-country skiing. Without really thinking about what I was doing, I stuffed the mittens, a warm knit cap he never wore, and a soft plaid scarf into my backpack. He had so many clothes I knew he'd never miss a few things.

Then I wrapped my scarf around my neck, jumped on my bike, and rode down the footpath toward the library.

"Hey, Mad Dog!"

I glanced to the right and waved to Keith and Julie. They were standing on one of the little bridges on a path leading to a tot lot. Keith was leaning against the railing and Julie was leaning against him, their arms around each other.

"Where are you going?" Keith wanted to know.

Without stopping, I yelled back at them, "The library."

"Bookworm!" Julie called after me, laughing.

"Better than a make-out artist," I mumbled to myself. She and Keith were really getting on my nerves with all this dumb romance stuff. Didn't they ever look at their parents? If that's where it got you — married and living in a place like Adelphia — kissing wasn't for me.

As I coasted down hills and swept around curves, I wanted to shout at the joggers and dog walkers, "Look at me, I'm Kelly McAllister!"

Like a little kid, I stood up to pedal so I could go even faster. The sun was shining, and the wind blew in my face, fresh and clean and cold, and I knew I would never give up the way Mom had, never. Not now, not when I was forty.

Zooming through the tunnel under Warfield Parkway, without pausing to read the graffiti, I pedaled uphill to the library. After locking my bike in the rack, I went to the reference room. Mr. Weems was there, half asleep over an open book, and Mr. Carter was sitting at the information desk.

Mr. Carter gave me a look which said I'd better behave myself; he's never forgotten the time he caught me making prints of my face, hands, and rear end on the copying machine. From the way he carried on, you'd think I'd pulled my jeans down and mooned the whole library, which, of course, I hadn't. It was the texture of my Levi's that interested me, not my bare bottom.

Anyway, I waggled my fingers at him and gave him a little grin. Then I sat down across from Mr. Weems. I could feel Mr. Carter's eyes boring into me, so I pulled a sketchbook out of my backpack and set to work drawing Mr. Weems. I didn't dare offer him lunch till I was sure Mr. Carter had lost interest in me. I'd been caught eating in the library several times, and I knew there was no quicker way to get kicked out. Librarians have a real nose for food. Just the rattle of a bag alerts them.

Half an hour and three sketches later, Mr. Carter was replaced by Miss McCarthy. As soon as she was engrossed in her book, I cleared my throat and leaned toward Mr. Weems. He was awake now, and he'd already checked me out with his little telescope. "Are you hungry?" I whispered.

Without looking at me, he shook his head and fluttered his hands at me.

"I brought you some good food," I persisted. "I fixed it myself."

He kept his head bent over his book and fluttered his hands again.

"You can't eat in here." I pulled the grocery bag out of my backpack and set it down in front of him. "You have to take it outside, but I can watch your things while you're gone."

He looked at me then. His eyes were pure blue, the color of a June sky, but I felt like Gandalf confronting a terrified mouse. Again he shook his head and pushed the bag away.

"There's other stuff in it." I shoved the bag toward him again. "Clothes. You know, mittens and things."

But he wouldn't look at me or the bag. He just hunched his shoulders so they rose up around his ears and sat absolutely still. He reminded me of one of those monkeys, "See no evil, hear no evil, speak no evil."

"Kelly, my God, what are you doing?" It was Courtney, hissing in my ear like a goose.

"Go away." I must have spoken louder than I meant to because a man at a nearby table glared at me.

"Will you keep your voice down?" the man said. "Some people come here to study," he added in a carrying voice which reached Miss McCarthy's ears.

She looked up from her book, obviously annoyed at

being interrupted. "You girls behave yourselves!" she said.

"I wasn't doing anything," Courtney said indignantly.

"Me either," I added quickly.

"What did I tell you the other day?" Mrs. Martin stepped out of an office behind Miss McCarthy and frowned at me. "Pick up your things and get out of here. You too," she said to Courtney.

"Me?" Courtney's face flushed. "What did I do?"

"I have eyes." Mrs. Martin folded her arms across her chest and fixed us both with an I-hate-teenagers look.

"Whose is this?" Mrs. Martin asked as I started to leave without the grocery bag.

"His," I said and kept going, afraid that Mr. Weems would jump up and deny it.

Courtney followed me down the steps. "You really make me mad, Kelly McAllister," she said, her voice louder than usual. "I had a lot of work to do, and my mother's not coming to pick me up till four o'clock. What am I going to do for the next two hours?"

"How should I know?" I stopped and glared at her. "It's your own fault for butting your nose into my business. I told you I have to interview Mr. Weems, and just when I thought I was getting somewhere you had to come along and mess it all up!"

"Well, excuse me." Courtney made an effort to be sarcastic, but I ignored her.

"Where are you going?" she asked as I walked away.

I shrugged. "What's it to you?"

"Want to go to the mall?"

As I hesitated, Courtney lingered in the lobby, frowning at me. She was still mad, I knew that, but she hated going anywhere by herself. Especially the mall. Nobody went there alone.

"Might as well," I said. Without looking at her, I slung my backpack over my shoulder and walked through the tunnel ahead of Courtney, leaving my bike chained to the library rack. What else was there to do?

The mall was crowded with shoppers already thinking about Christmas in the middle of November. A crew of workmen were building Santa's village in front of Hecht's department store, while another group set up a tiny tot train in front of the Woodward and Lothrop store at the opposite end of the mall. The sound of their hammers punctuated the piped-in happytime music and the wails of babies in strollers.

The Eatery was mobbed, and we were lucky to find a table after we'd gotten sodas and hamburgers at Roy Rogers'.

Courtney sipped her Coke and stared at the people walking past. "Look at them." She pointed at a group of older kids. The guys were wearing enormous overcoats from Goodwill and their hair stuck up in spikes. The girls with them had half their heads shaved and wore baggy black clothes and little pointy-toed boots. "They think they're so cool."

I looked at Courtney. Her brown hair was long and wavy and she wore big glasses with pale frames; unlike me, she bought her clothes brand-new, and she always looked shiny clean and neat. Today she was wearing a long pink sweater over a white turtleneck, and her jeans had an expensive label where you couldn't miss seeing it.

"I think they're kind of interesting," I said, more to annoy her than anything else. "At least you notice them."

Courtney raised her eyebrows and her glasses slid down her pointed nose. "I suppose you'll dye your hair purple next," she said. "You already dress nearly that bad anyway."

"It's a wonder you aren't embarrassed to come to the mall with me," I said. I ate the pickle, all that was left of my burger, and tried to coax a little more soda out of the ice in my cup.

Courtney sighed. "I keep hoping this is just some weird stage you're going through."

"Don't hold your breath, Court."

"Come on," she said. "Let's go shopping."

"For what?" I followed her into the Hitching Post. "I wouldn't waste my money in here," I said, but Courtney wasn't listening.

"Can I help you find anything?" a salesgirl asked Courtney. She was wearing an outfit she must have bought in the store. It looked nice on her, but why spend a hundred dollars when you can get funky stuff for almost nothing at Goodwill?

"We're just looking." Courtney smiled in the same fake way the salesgirl was smiling. They were practically smirking at each other, and I turned away, embarrassed. Just going into the Hitching Post made me feel uncomfortable, and I wished Courtney would leave instead of letting the salesgirl lead her farther into the store.

"Everything on this rack is twenty-five percent off." The salesgirl grabbed the sleeve of a big, fluffy sweater and held it up. "This color would look great on you."

Courtney considered the sweater. It was a hideous shade of magenta. She and the salesgirl exchanged more smirks. "It's beautiful," Courtney said, "but it doesn't go with anything I own."

"The skirts are on sale too." Still grinning, the salesgirl held up a plaid skirt with the same ugly color in it.

Courtney shook her head and started edging away. "No, thanks, not today." She wasn't smiling now, so I said, "God, Courtney, your mother! We're supposed to meet her!"

Safely out of the store, Courtney started laughing. "Thanks, Kelly. I thought we'd never get away from that girl. Did you ever see such an ugly sweater?"

I wanted to tell her we could have escaped easily if she'd told the salesgirl what she thought about the sweater in the first place, but I knew she wouldn't understand. She'd just get mad or something and accuse me of criticizing her.

"Let's go to Fashion Unlimited," Courtney suggested, and reluctantly I followed her. I swear we wandered around the mall for hours, going from one clothing store to another. I was so bored, I finally left her in the Gap dressing room where she was trying on a dozen pairs of jeans, but she found me next door in McDonald's buying a Coke.

She was just about to get mad when she saw Dennis Cooper loping along ahead of us with three of his friends. Dennis is tall and dark, and he always looks cool. You know — he wears his denim jacket three sizes too big and it's faded to just the right shade of soft blue. As if that weren't enough, he's also the captain of the basketball team, and lots of girls are madly in love with him, including Courtney, excluding me. He's a conceited jock, if you ask me .

"Come on, Kelly." Courtney ran up the steps behind Dennis. "Let's see where he's going." Her face was all red and she was giggling and shushing me at the same time.

Although I was embarrassed, I followed Courtney, hoping Dennis wouldn't notice us. He was a senior, for heaven's sake. He'd think Courtney and I were dumb little dweebs if he guessed what we were doing.

Luckily for both of us, Dennis and his friends left the mall without seeing Courtney and me. On the way out, though, he dropped a gum wrapper which Courtney pounced on.

"I'll keep it forever, Kelly," she whispered as she tucked it into her wallet. I just rolled my eyes.

Finally it was time to walk back to the library so Courtney could meet her mother. "She'll never know I was at the mall," she said smugly as we stood in the lobby watching for her mother's car.

When Mrs. Andrews pulled up, the station wagon was packed with Courtney's little brother's ice hockey team. We could hear them yelling before we even opened the library door.

I watched Courtney get in the front seat, fending off her brother's hockey stick. What a relief to be by myself again. How could my dad think Courtney was so great? Just because she got good grades didn't mean she was smart. No intelligent person could enjoy shopping the way she did. At the rate she was going, she'd soon be as bad as Julie's mother, spending all her spare time at the mall.

Tightening my scarf to keep the wind from blowing down my neck, I went to the rack and unlocked my bike. I sat on it for a few minutes, trying to decide what to do. I wanted to know if Mr. Weems had eaten the sandwich and taken the clothes, but Mrs. Martin wouldn't let me come inside till tomorrow. That was one of her rules — you were always kicked out for a whole day.

Glancing at my watch, I saw it was four-fifteen. The library closed at five on Saturdays. If I hung around till then, I'd see Mr. Weems. Maybe he'd thank me for the sandwiches and clothes, I thought, maybe he'd even talk to me. Whether he knew it or not, he needed a friend like me who could help him and understand him.

As the wind tugged at my clothes, I hunched my shoulders to keep warm and watched the people slowly leave the library.

Chapter 7

BY FIVE O'CLOCK, my feet felt as if they were fro-
zen to the ground. The library was emptying fast
— teenagers, little kids, older people. At last, Mr.
Weems appeared, his face almost hidden by my father's
cross-country ski hat with reindeer knit into the wool
and a little tassel on top.

He was also wearing the mittens and the scarf. They
made his old down parka look all the more scruffy, but
I knew they would help keep him warm.

As I watched, he stopped beside a trash can and
carefully set down his plastic bags. Then he opened the
sack I'd left on the table. He took out a sandwich and
unwrapped it. Lifting up the top piece of bread, he
poked at the meat, cheese, tomatoes, and lettuce. Then
he sniffed it, hesitated a moment, and dumped it into
the trash. To my disappointment, he did the same

thing with the other two sandwiches. It was like watching my mother go through my trick-or-treat loot, making sure it was safe to eat.

I wanted to snatch the sandwiches out of the trash can and tell him how good they were, but I stayed where I was, thinking he'd at least eat the fruit.

He examined the bananas and the oranges carefully, sniffing, squeezing, peeling back the skin. Then each one went into the trash with a thump that made my insides hurt.

After that, he opened the thermos and sniffed the coffee. Making a face, he poured it out, but he opened one of his bags and stuffed my Wonder Woman thermos inside. All that was left was the V–8 juice. He looked it over, shook it a few times, and dropped it into his pocket. Then he hoisted his bags and walked away from me, taking a path that led to Lake Columbus.

I wheeled my bike after him, too upset to say anything. He didn't know me, I told myself, not really. To him, I was just another teenager, laughing at him or trying to hurt him. Like Mom at Halloween, he was probably afraid I'd poisoned the sandwiches or stuck razor blades in the fruit. It made me feel terrible to think he'd have such a low opinion of me, but at least he was wearing the clothes. That was something, wasn't it?

Without looking back, Mr. Weems kept on toward the lake. Despite the obvious weight of his bags, he walked fast, and I had to hurry to keep him in sight.

By the time we reached Town Centre, it was dark. The lights on the pier shone in the black water, and their reflections shivered as the wind rippled the lake's surface. Not far from shore, the swans, ducks, and geese bobbed gently, their heads tucked under their wings.

If it had been a summer evening, we would have been surrounded by boys on skateboards, little kids running and shouting, parents with babies in strollers and backpacks, teenagers like Julie and me, joggers, and dog walkers. But in November, Mr. Weems and I had the lake to ourselves. The only people in sight were sitting in Mister Charlie's restaurant, eating and gazing out the windows like diners on a train.

Mr. Weems walked steadily without looking up from the path. When I realized he was heading away from the office buildings and restaurants of Town Centre, I stopped and watched him vanish into the dark woods at the end of the lake. Some bad things have happened to women on the footpaths at night, and I didn't want to risk following Mr. Weems any farther.

As I pedaled toward home with the wind in my face, I wondered where Mr. Weems was going to sleep. The temperature was probably already in the thirties. I remembered how cold I'd been when I went camping with my scout troop; we'd gone in September and even then I'd been miserable all night. Maybe you got used to it, sleeping outside, but it was hard to imagine enjoying it.

*

The next day my father decided to take Mom and me out for Sunday brunch. "Where would you like to go?" he asked Mom.

"How about Mister Charlie's?" Mom suggested. "It has a nice view of the lake, and it's buffet style so you can eat as much as you want."

As we were getting ready to leave the house, Dad said, "You're not planning to wear that outfit, are you?"

I looked down at my sweater, another thrift shop treasure, several sizes too big and out at both elbows. My jeans, the very ones I preserved on the copy machine, had matching holes in both knees. "What's wrong with it?"

He sighed. "You must have something in one piece that fits you."

After a long and futile argument which began with my clothes and rapidly escalated to my grades, the state of my room, and my attitude in general, I finally ended up wearing my standard brunch outfit — a shapeless gray Laura Ashley jumper, a black turtleneck, black tights, and lace-up granny boots.

From the expression on his face, I knew Dad wasn't crazy about this outfit or the rhinestone earrings hanging halfway to my shoulders or the army jacket and scarf I put on before we left the house. To silence himself, he lit his pipe and led us to the car. Like Courtney, he was probably hoping I was just going through a weird stage.

Mister Charlie's was crowded with people eagerly

helping themselves to scrambled eggs, sausages, bacon, fried potatoes, pancakes, waffles, fresh fruit, pastries, and a lot of unbreakfast things like beef stroganoff and chicken tetrazzini. Through the steamed up windows, you could see Lake Columbus, gray water under a gray sky streaked with thick clouds.

We settled ourselves at a table with a view of the lake. While Dad talked to Mom about some boring case he was working on, I ate my pancakes and watched the ducks and geese diving for the popcorn a woman and her children were tossing to them.

As I was thinking about going back to the buffet for a second helping, I saw Mr. Weems trudging along beside the lake, carrying his bags and wearing Dad's tasseled ski cap. Although I hoped neither of my parents would see him, I heard Mom ask Dad, "Is that the man you and Kelly were talking about?"

Dad stared out the window and frowned. "That's him, all right."

Mom shook her head. "What an awful way to live," she said. "He looks so cold, and those bags must be heavy."

"All he needs to do is clean himself up, get a haircut, and find a job," Dad muttered between mouthfuls of eggs Benedict.

"Doing what?" I stared at him.

"Washing dishes, scrubbing floors, how do I know?"

"What I don't understand," Mom said before I had a chance to argue with Dad, "is why he's here in Adelphia. If he were in Baltimore or Washington, he'd have a shelter to go to, meals, clothing."

"Maybe he'd even have a chauffeur to drive him to the library," Dad said.

Mom leaned across the table, her breakfast forgotten. "Don't be so sarcastic, Greg. You've heard Aunt Eliza talk about the people she's met at her soup kitchen in Baltimore. Many of them aren't much different from you and me. They've just run into some bad luck."

I watched Dad fork up a mouthful of fruit salad. "You know I admire your aunt," he said. "She's a wonderful woman, but she's too idealistic to see things as they are."

Mom frowned. "If she's too idealistic, then you're too cynical."

She turned her head to watch Mr. Weems disappear around a curve in the footpath. "Did you notice his hat, Greg?" she asked.

I held my breath as Dad shook his head.

"It was just like the one I bought you in Bar Harbor a few years ago. You know, the one with the reindeer."

Dad shrugged and craned his neck to get a glimpse of Mr. Weems, but he was out of sight. "I never did like that hat," Dad said and returned his attention to eating.

"Can I leave now?" I pushed my chair back.

"Leave?" Mom stared at me. "Don't you want seconds?"

"I'm stuffed." Patting my full stomach, I added, "The library opens in a few minutes and I need to get some books."

"Again?" Dad looked up from his plate.

"I told you, I have a big paper to work on."

"Should I pick you up?" Mom asked.

"It's a nice day. I can walk home." Leaving my parents to linger over a second cup of coffee, I cruised past the buffet and stuffed a handful of rolls into my pocket for the ducks.

Outside, the wind hit my face and I shivered as I ran down the path toward the lake, hoping to catch up with Mr. Weems. Ahead of me, the pier stretched out into the water. Two or three dozen mallard ducks bunched together near the shore while the swans swam around them like a king and queen protecting their loyal subjects. Undisturbed, the Canada geese floated in the middle of the lake, and the seagulls circled overhead, crying.

Mr. Weems was sitting at the end of the pier, his back to me. Cautiously I approached him and sat down near him. Without saying anything, I pulled one of the rolls out of my pocket. Breaking off a piece, I tossed it toward the ducks, and they swam toward me quacking loudly. More sedately, the swans followed, their necks arching gracefully. Overhead, the seagulls circled, squawking like quarrelsome children.

I glanced at Mr. Weems. He was observing me with his little handmade telescope. I grinned at him.

"They're really hungry," I said in a voice squeaky with nervousness.

He didn't say anything. Turning his head away from me, he huddled deeper into his jacket.

"I guess people don't feed them as much in the winter." I went on, "which is really weird because that's when they need food the most."

Still no answer. I might as well have been talking to myself. The wind rustled the plastic bags and stirred the tassel on his ski cap.

I tossed more bread to the ducks, trying to make sure they all got some. As a seagull dived and snatched a crust right out from under one of the slower ducks, I heard a little chuckle from Mr. Weems.

"The seagulls are real comedians, aren't they?" I glanced at him, eager to seize anything to start a conversation. "I love watching them fly. They're so graceful." I tilted my head back to watch a gull soar up into the sky and hover high above us. The weak sunlight shone through his feathers, touching them with ivory.

Mr. Weems didn't say anything. He kept his eyes on the ducks and ignored the gull wheeling over our heads.

"Here, swans, swans," I called to the two birds as they circled the crowd of ducks, gliding through the water so smoothly they scarcely made a ripple.

"Are you too proud to take anything?" I asked them. Out of the corner of my eye, I saw Mr. Weems nod as if he were speaking for the swans. Then he stood up, gathered his bags, and walked away, his feet soundless on the boards.

Tossing the last of my bread at the ducks, I hurried after him. "Are you going to the library now?" I asked him.

Head bent, he ignored me.

"If you're hungry, I could treat you to something at the mall," I said.

Mr. Weems just trudged along, and I had to hurry to keep up with him. His nose, the only visible part of his face, was bright red with cold.

"You didn't eat what I brought you yesterday. Maybe you don't like sandwiches, and I didn't know if you put cream in your coffee or not, but if we went to the mall, you could get whatever you want." I knew I was babbling, but I was so worried about him. He had to eat something. He'd starve if he didn't.

Mr. Weems shook his head and walked faster, forcing me to run to keep up with him.

"I just want to be your friend," I shouted at him. "I want to help you, that's all!"

Mr. Weems stopped so suddenly I almost bumped into him. Fixing me with a hard stare, he said, "Don't need no friends, don't need help." His voice rose. "Just leave me be!"

By now we were at the main entrance to the library. Without saying another word or acknowledging my presence in any way, Mr. Weems pushed through the glass doors, struggling briefly with his bags, and climbed the stairs to the reference room. As he paused to adjust his load, a woman passed him. She stared at him as if he weren't quite human and hurried down the stairs, giving him a wide berth.

Dumping a stack of paperback romances on the counter, she frowned at the clerk standing under the check-out sign. "I can't understand why you let that man in here," she said.

The clerk shrugged as he began stamping her books. "The library is a public building," he said. "We can't discriminate against people."

"That's ridiculous. I'm a taxpayer, and I shouldn't have to put up with somebody like him."

"That's right." A middle-aged man joined the woman. "He doesn't belong in here."

The clerk kept his head bent over the pile of books the man had slammed down on the counter. "May I have your card, sir?" he asked.

The man sighed and extracted his card from his wallet. "He could be a psychopath," he said. "The kind who pulls out a gun and shoots everybody in sight."

The woman gasped and clutched her books to her chest. "Good lord, I never thought of that."

"I've written a letter to the director." The man drew himself up very straight and adjusted his tie. "Perhaps he'll take some action."

I glared at the man. Never had I hated anybody as much as I hated him at that moment. As he turned away from the desk, I stepped in front of him. "Just where is Mr. Weems supposed to go?" I asked.

He stared at me, taking in every detail of my appearance with obvious distaste. "That's his problem," he said coldly.

"Do you want him to go off and freeze to death in a gutter so you won't have to see him?" My heart was beating fast and I was having trouble breathing, but I wanted to make this man see what an awful person he was. "He has just as much right to be here as you have."

The man shifted his books, and I noticed their titles — *How to Make a Fortune on the Stock Market, Smart Investing, Financial Planning for the Eighties.* Giving me a look that clearly expressed his opinion, he swept through the glass doors behind the lady with the romances.

The clerk stared after them and shook his head. "People like that make me so mad," he said.

"I hope the stock market crashes again, and he loses all his money," I said. "Then maybe he'll find out what it's like to be Mr. Weems."

The clerk nodded his head in agreement, and I ran upstairs to the reference room, hoping Mrs. Martin wouldn't be at the information desk. I really wanted to talk to Mr. Weems. He needed somebody on his side. Otherwise he might get kicked out of the library. With the coldest part of winter still to come, he had to have a warm place to go.

Chapter 8

I SAT DOWN at Mr. Weems's table, but, even though Mrs. Martin wasn't there, I couldn't get a word out of him. No matter what I said or did, he just fluttered his hands like somebody shooing a cat away. After half an hour of rejection, I got discouraged and went down to the children's room to talk to Mrs. Hunter.

"Do many people complain about Mr. Weems?" I asked her.

She looked up from her book and sighed. "We were talking about him at a staff meeting the other day," she said. "According to Dorothy Martin, the director has received dozens of letters about him. She and the other reference room librarians put up with complaints every day, and so do the clerks at the circulation desk."

"But doesn't anybody care about him? Don't they worry about where he sleeps and what he eats?"

"A few people have tried to help him, but he won't let anybody near him," she said.

I picked up one of the pens on her desk and started doodling on a piece of scratch paper. "Is the library going to kick him out?"

"It depends on the director," Mrs. Hunter said. "He makes the final decisions."

"All Mr. Weems wants is a warm, quiet place to read. If he can't come to the library, where will he go?"

"We've gotten in touch with a clinic," she said. "They're sending a social worker here tomorrow to talk to Mr. Weems, to find out how he's living and let him know about their services. They can do more for him than we can, Kelly. He needs professional help."

I bent my head over a sketch of Mr. Weems and worked on shading in his bushy beard, tangles and all. "He told me he didn't want any friends or any help," I said.

"He spoke to you?"

"That's all he said. Hardly what I'd call a conversation." I sat back and eyed my drawing, thinking I'd made Mr. Weems look too much like one of the seven dwarfs.

"My, that's a wonderful likeness." Mrs. Hunter's long hair fell to one side as she tipped her head and studied the sketch.

I shrugged, letting the compliment slip past. People who can't draw always think it's wonderful when I sketch something. They just don't realize the difference between what I can do and what a real artist can do.

"I think it would be awful if the library kicked him out," I said. "Just because a few old middle-class tax-payers don't like seeing him here."

"Oh, Kelly." Mrs. Hunter smiled at me and gave my shoulder a little squeeze.

"It's not fair." I frowned at Mrs. Hunter. "Some people have everything and other people don't even have a place to live. What kind of country is this?"

"Excuse me, miss." A man pushed a little kid toward Mrs. Hunter. "Tell the librarian what you want, Jeff."

Jeff looked up at his father. "You tell her," he whispered.

"Oh, no." The man shook his head vigorously. "You're the one with the homework assignment, not me. You tell her."

"Can I help you?" Mrs. Hunter leaned across the desk and smiled sympathetically at Jeff who was still begging his father to do the talking.

Leaving her to help the poor kid, I decided to go home. It was almost time for dinner, and I was sure I wouldn't get anything more out of Mr. Weems today.

*

The next day in English class, we were reading about Achilles' return to battle after his friend's death; to avenge Patroklos, he was splitting people's heads in two, hewing arms from bodies, driving his chariot through rivers of blood. Every time Homer described another skull bursting, all the girls in the room made sick noises, and the boys cheered.

"Achilles is just like Rambo," Brett Phillips whispered to me, but I ignored him. If there's one thing I hate, it's people who think killing is great.

"I've run off some war poems on the mimeograph," Mr. Hardy said. "Take a few minutes to read them, and then we'll contrast them with the *Iliad*."

At the mention of poetry, a lot of the kids groaned, but the whole class got quiet after Mr. Hardy had given out all the sheets. The first poem was called "Dulce et Decorum Est," by Wilfred Owen. It was packed with images of death and destruction and horror, and it made you feel what it was like to be marching through mud with guns going off all around you and people dying. Unlike Homer, Wilfred Owen didn't think anybody was going to win any honors or become a great hero. He seemed to be saying all the men were suffering and dying for nothing.

The last lines of the poem were aimed at politicians who sent young men to war, Mr. Hardy said; if the politicians knew what war was really like, they wouldn't tell the young men it was good and proper to die for their country because they'd realize it was a lie.

Brett Phillips raised his hand before Mr. Hardy had finished. "Was this written by some Vietnam protester?" he asked scornfully. As usual, Brett was wearing his camouflage shirt and trousers. He and his friends play war all the time with plastic submachine guns. He told me once he was ready for the next war, in fact he could hardly wait.

"Wilfred Owen was killed in World War One," Mr.

Hardy said. "He wrote his poetry on the battlefield, and if it sounds angry, it's meant to."

Then he read us a few lines from another of Owen's poems, "Mental Cases":

Always they must see these things and hear them,
Batter of guns and shatter of flying muscles,
Carnage incomparable, and human squander,
Rucked too thick for these men's extrication.

"What does that make you think of?" he asked.

"Vietnam veterans," I said, "the ones who just can't forget all the awful things they saw and did."

"You mean it's been like that in other wars?" Keith asked. "I thought Vietnam vets were the only ones messed up."

Mr. Hardy shook his head. "Look at 'Repression of War Experience' by Siegfried Sassoon," he said.

Sassoon's poem was a little easier to read than Owen's because the language was more up to date, but it was just as sad. It was about a man who can't stop thinking about the war. Everything he sees reminds him of it. He says he won't go crazy if he can control his thoughts, but he sees moths flying into the candle's flame and that reminds him of soldiers dying. Even though he's safe at home, he hears the guns in France.

Hark! Thud, thud, thud—quite soft . . .
*   they never cease—*

*Those whispering guns—O Christ, I want to go
   out
And screech at them to stop—I'm going crazy;
I'm going stark, staring mad because of the guns.*

"Was he in World War One too?" Courtney asked.

"Yes, but he lived through it," Mr. Hardy said. "A lot of his generation weren't so lucky."

"But if you read his other poems," I ran my finger down the page. "'The Troops' is about young men dying, and 'They' is about some dumb bishop who thinks the veterans will come back changed because of the honor they won, but the soldiers know they'll be changed because they're wounded and dying, and look at this one, 'In the Pink.'"

I paused and glanced at Brett, daring him to say anything. Then I read the last two lines out loud:

*Tonight he's in the pink; but soon he'll die.
And still the war goes on; he doesn't know why.*

Keith was staring at me, but I kept on talking. "Well, you can see that Sassoon probably never got over the war," I said. "No matter how long he lived, he must have remembered it every day of his life. How does any soldier forget killing people or seeing his friends die all around him?"

In the pause before Mr. Hardy answered, I thought about Mr. Weems. He had seen and done awful things, he had witnessed "multitudinous murders" like the mental cases in Wilfred Owen's poem. No wonder he couldn't live an ordinary life.

"People force themselves to forget the bad things, Kelly," Mr. Hardy said. "Otherwise they couldn't function."

"Maybe if they remembered them, we wouldn't have any more wars," I said.

"Kelly's right," Keith said. "That's what Wilfred Owen and Sassoon are trying to say. Old men forget what war is like, so they make up lies about honor and glory and trick young men into fighting. And the young men die, not the old men."

"That's just what the Russians want us to think." Brett leaned toward Keith, his face reddening with anger. "We could've made Vietnam into a parking lot if it hadn't been for bleeding hearts like you. I don't think we should read poems by a bunch of cowards. I'm ready to defend my country. I'll die if I have to."

"Then you're even dumber than I thought," I told Brett. I glanced at "Dulce et Decorum Est." "You're a child 'ardent for some desperate glory,'" I quoted.

"That's enough," Mr. Hardy interrupted Brett who was opening his mouth to make a comeback. "Let's not descend to the personal level, kids."

"Well, where were you during the war?" Brett asked Mr. Hardy. "In Canada or Sweden?"

"I was on a helicopter base," Mr. Hardy said quietly.

"You flew a Huey?" Brian Adams asked, obviously impressed.

Mr. Hardy shook his head. "Repaired them."

"Was everybody really stoned all the time over there?" Jason Lombardi wanted to know.

Mr. Hardy ran a hand over his beard. "Let's get back to the *Iliad*, now," he said. "Do you see any evidence that Homer didn't think war was all glory?"

While Courtney tried to answer Mr. Hardy's question, I slumped down in my seat and tuned her out. If Vietnam had ruined Mr. Weems's life, what had it done to my dad? He didn't seem to have any problems, but he couldn't have forgotten about it, not really.

He'd only been twenty when he went to Vietnam, not much older than Keith. Just thinking about my dad firing a gun made me shiver. It was hard to imagine him killing somebody, but he must have.

And people must have shot at him too. Suppose he'd been killed? I wouldn't be sitting in this classroom talking about wars I'd never witnessed. I wouldn't exist.

As Mr. Hardy began summarizing our discussion, I stared around the room at Keith and Brett and the other boys, some of them for war, others against it, and tried to imagine my dad at their age, skateboarding and playing basketball, lifeguarding in the summer at a neighborhood swimming pool, going to Ocean City on weekends with his friends, cruising the street for girls on Saturday nights.

And then, when he was just a little older, going off to Vietnam, half a world away, fighting people who hadn't ever had a childhood. Just war every day of their lives.

I couldn't see Keith or even Brett, not the way I knew them now, going to war and then coming home as if nothing had happened. Was my father hard and cold and insensitive? Or was he brave in a way I couldn't imagine?

*

When class was over, Mr. Hardy asked me to stay a minute. "That's the most you've said all year, Kelly," he said.

"Usually I hate poetry," I said. "Except for Shel Silverstein, I've never read any I liked. All those dumb rhymes and artificial words and stuff. But these poems, they make you think."

Mr. Hardy smiled. "That's the purpose of all good literature."

"But people like Brett. He didn't even try to understand the poems. He just wants to think war is all hero stuff."

"Let's hope he never finds out what it's really like." Mr. Hardy took off his glasses and polished the lens with his handkerchief. His face looked young and sort of defenseless without them. "Anyway, thanks for having some good things to say, Kelly. Try to keep it up, will you?"

I nodded, happy he was pleased. "I was afraid you were mad at me for calling Brett dumb," I told him as I lingered in the doorway.

"Well, that wasn't real cool," he said. "Name calling is the easy way out, you know. What's hard is to make people see why they're wrong."

As I thought about that, the bell for sixth period rang and I had to run down the hall to Mr. Poland's class where I got a lecture on tardiness and more questions about my current issues paper. If only Mr. Hardy taught all my classes!

Chapter 9

WHEN SCHOOL WAS finally over, I saw Julie and Keith waiting for me by my locker. As usual, they had their arms around each other's waists. If they hadn't already seen me coming, I would've hidden in the girls' room until I was sure they'd gone home. I didn't feel like tagging along with them, watching them steal kisses when they thought I wasn't looking.

"Hey, Kelly," Keith said. "You were great in English today."

I shrugged and concentrated on spinning the dial on my combination lock. "Brett's such a jerk."

"He's kind of cute, though." Julie giggled and ducked away from Keith as he tousled her hair. "Just kidding, just kidding," she told him.

"I really liked those poems," Keith went on, holding Julie in some sort of hammerlock he learned in wrestling while she squirmed and giggled and struck at him with her fists.

"Me too." I tried to ignore Julie's squeals, but it's hard to have an intelligent conversation with somebody when he's wrestling with his girl friend.

"Sorry? Sorry?" Keith eased up on Julie and she broke away, still laughing.

"Look what you did to my hair, you idiot." Pulling out her comb and pocket mirror, Julie went to work on herself, and Keith turned back to me.

"I sure hope we never have another war," he said as we walked down the hall. "I can't imagine going through stuff like that, killing other people, knowing they'll kill you if you don't get them first."

"Don't worry," I said. "They'll just drop a couple of atomic bombs this time and nuke us all to nothing."

"Oh, Kelly." Julie frowned at me. "Save it for English class. War's too depressing to talk about."

"Well, of course it's depressing," Keith said.

"Unless you're Brett Phillips," I said. "Then it's a chance to prove how brave you are."

"Or how dumb you are," Keith added.

"Or how dead you are," I finished.

"Come on, you guys." Julie kissed Keith. "Let's go to the mall. I'm starving."

"Julie, sometimes you have to think about things," I said. "Even if they *are* depressing."

Julie tossed her hair, and I brushed it away from my face, suddenly angry at her. "I only get to live once," she said, "and I want to have fun."

"You sound like a character on a TV show," I said. "One of the dumb ones everybody laughs at."

"Thanks a lot!" Julie glared at me. "At least I don't go around dressed like some sort of junior freak bumming everybody out all the time."

"Hey," Keith said, pulling away from both of us, "what's the matter with you two?"

"Nothing's the matter with *me*." Julie grabbed Keith's jacket and pulled him toward her, leaving me standing alone.

Turning my back, I walked away from them, afraid I was going to cry. It was one thing for Courtney to criticize my clothes, but Julie was supposed to be my best friend and it really hurt to hear mean things from her. Since when had she thought I was a junior freak? Just last week we'd been laughing and carrying on, and now she was calling me names and claiming I bummed her out. As tears pricked at the back of my eyes, I shoved my fists deep into my pockets and walked faster, getting madder with each step.

If she thought I was going to buy a new wardrobe at the Hitching Post and priss around in designer jeans and sixty-dollar shoes just to please her, she was wrong. Let Julie Sinclair spend the rest of her life chasing Keith and laughing at everything. I had more important things to do. I didn't need her anymore. Or Keith either.

But still, when I got to the door at the end of the hall, I paused for just a second and took a quick look over my shoulder. I was thinking Keith, at least, might be coming after me. But the long hall stretched away from me in perfect vanishing point perspective. No one was in sight except a janitor pushing a mop.

I left school half-running, half-walking, heading toward the library. Maybe Mr. Weems would talk to me today, maybe he'd see we were a lot alike after all. Two outcasts, friendless, alone, misunderstood, jeered at. Letting my imagination go berserk, I saw Mr. Weems and me leaving Adelphia together, turning our backs on the people who hated us. We'd hit the road, he and I, ride the rails like old-time hoboes, see America from sea to shining sea. We'd be free, and we wouldn't care what people like Julie and my father thought of us.

By the time I got to the library, I was out of breath from running, and my side ached, but I was sure today was the day Mr. Weems would decide to be my friend. Trying not to attract Mr. Carter's attention, I walked quietly into the reference room. Mr. Weems was dozing over a book, but he looked at me when I sat down at a nearby table. I smiled and waved at him, but he just bent his head and hunched his shoulders like a turtle pulling into his shell.

While I was thinking of something to say, a neatly dressed man walked into the reference room and sat down at Mr. Weems's table. He introduced himself as Dave Walker from social services, but Mr. Weems didn't look up from his book.

Although I did my best to hear every word, Mr. Walker spoke very softly. Keeping his head bent over his book, Mr. Weems responded with little waving-away gestures. Every now and then he mumbled something, and Mr. Walker leaned toward him, nodding as if he were trying hard to understand.

Finally Mr. Walker stood up and closed his briefcase. He looked defeated, I thought. "If you change your mind, let me know," he said to Mr. Weems. "As a veteran, you're entitled to certain benefits, and I'd like to help you get them. Nobody has to live like you do."

For the first time, Mr. Weems looked at Mr. Walker. "I like the way I live," he said very clearly. "It's my own free choice. I don't need nothing from nobody."

Mr. Walker sighed as if he thought Mr. Weems was deceiving himself. "At least take my card." He held it out, and, when Mr. Weems didn't take it, he laid it down on the table and said, "I was in Vietnam myself, you know. It's not easy for any of us."

Mr. Walker hesitated for a moment, waiting for Mr. Weems to respond. "Call me if you change your mind," he added. Then he said good-bye and turned away.

I knew how Mr. Walker felt. It was obvious he was really worried about Mr. Weems and wanted to help him, but he couldn't get through. Mr. Weems didn't trust him any more than he trusted me or anybody else.

While I watched, Mr. Weems made his little telescope and looked through it as Mr. Walker left the reference room. Then he peeked at me before returning his attention to his book.

Bending my head over a new drawing, I worked hard at shading in the details of Mr. Weems's face, trying to catch the haunted expression in his eyes. I wanted to make him look like an eagle, wounded but eager to escape his bonds and soar again, but I couldn't get past his sadness, his loneliness. The face I drew looked more pathetic than tragic; it wasn't a face that dared to fly.

Closing my sketch pad, I opened my composition book and wrote a note.

Dear Mr. Weems,

I know you didn't want to talk to the social worker, but won't you please talk to me? I've got some bread for the ducks, so I'll wait for you on the pier at Town Centre. I really want to be your friend.

Yours truly,
Kelly McAllister

Glancing at Mr. Carter to make sure he wasn't looking, I folded the paper carefully into a small square and walked over to Mr. Weems. I paused, hoping he might look up. When he didn't, I put the note beside his book and walked away.

Outside, the wind had picked up and the sun was low in the sky. I shivered as I ran down the path toward the lake. Would he come? Or would he dump my note in the trash?

Like Sunday, I had the pier pretty much to myself. I sat down on a post at the end and watched the ducks swim toward me. As usual, the swans flanked them, their necks arched regally. Farther out, the Canada geese bobbed like toys on the water, and the seagulls circled overhead watching me for signs of food.

After half an hour, my rear end was chilled to the bone and my feet ached with cold. The ducks had given up on me and were diving for food in the lake while the swans circled languidly, giving the impression they were above hunger. The water itself had turned pink, reflecting the sky, and I knew it would be dark soon.

As I stood up to leave, I saw Mr. Weems trudging toward me. I sat back down, suddenly afraid. I hadn't thought he would come, not really, and now that he was actually taking a seat on the post next to mine, I didn't know what to say.

Uneasily I took the loaf of bread I'd brought to school out of my backpack and handed him a slice. Without looking at him, I tore a piece off another slice and tossed it to the ducks. As they dove for it, I saw another chunk splash into the water, and I knew Mr. Weems was feeding the ducks too.

For several minutes, we threw bread to the ducks and the swans. The seagulls wheeled around us, snatching pieces out of the air, fighting over each morsel, and losing most of it to the ducks.

After a while, the geese approached us, hoping to get their share. When the swans saw them, they raised their wings, stretched their necks, and swam rapidly toward them, their plumage gleaming in the rosy light of the setting sun. To my surprise, most of the geese retreated. The few who didn't were pursued by the swans until they too withdrew.

Triumphantly, the swans sailed back toward us and rejoined the ducks, leaving the geese to dive for weeds.

"I didn't know swans were so fierce," I said.

"This lake's their territory," Mr. Weems said. "They're defending it."

I stared at him, surprised he'd spoken. "But they don't mind the ducks being here," I said. Afraid I'd scare him if I looked at him, I watched the geese huddle together on the other side of the lake.

He shrugged. "Ducks are just little things. Swans don't care nothing about them. Geese are big, though, like them, so they got to fight them."

I stole a look at him, hoping he'd say more, but he was staring at the geese.

"Got any more bread?" he asked at last.

"One slice." I handed it to him, and he tore it in half.

"You take this piece." He crumbled his into little bits and tossed each one separately to the ducks. "That's all, boys." He dropped the last of the bread into the water. "No more today."

I scattered mine in an arc and watched the gulls dive at it, screaming at each other.

"Your name's Kelly?" Mr. Weems stared at me, his eyes almost hidden by Dad's ski cap.

I nodded, still too shy to ask him any questions.

"How come you want to be my friend? Is it some joke you and them other kids thought up?"

"No, it's not a joke." But I couldn't think of anything else to say. Unable to meet his eyes, I stared at the sky. The bright oranges and reds were fading now, turning grayish pink and purple, and a half moon hung low in the sky, just above the treetops.

"I'm just worried about you, that's all," I said at last. "Winter's coming, and you don't have anyplace to keep warm except the library."

Like me, Mr. Weems was gazing across the lake at the sky. He was as still as one of those little gnomes people buy for their gardens. "What's it to you?" he asked.

"I'm scared you'll freeze to death or something," I whispered.

"I like the cold," he said. "These sacks, they're full of warm stuff. A sleeping bag, blankets, I get along fine."

"But how about food?" I wanted to ask about the sandwiches and the fruit he'd thrown away, but I didn't want him to think I was criticizing him.

"I don't take nothing from nobody, I get what I want from dumpsters." He paused and glanced at me. "People eat too much, use too much heat, it's all waste, waste. Someday it'll all be gone, nothing left for nobody." For emphasis, I guess, he spit into the lake.

The water lapped against the pilings, and a seagull cried as it flew over our heads. "I seen the way the world will end," he whispered, and his voice sent a chill right through me, right down to my bones. "I seen death and destruction and the whole earth burned black, nothing left alive. I seen bodies with holes in them like Swiss cheese, blowed apart like they was never real. I seen a whole jungle burned and a little town and all the people killed. And when I look at this — " He waved his hand at the lake and Town Centre. "I see them tall buildings in pieces on the ground and all the windows busted and bodies scattered everywhere, women and children, kids like you. It don't matter where you live or what you have, nothing will save you. Nothing."

I sat still as stone, staring at him, seeing what he saw.

"Once I was your age," he went on. "And there was this war in a place I never heard of and it was still going on when I got out of high school. I was just a dumb kid and I wanted to do something for my country, you know, for Uncle Sam, so I joined the army. They was going to train me to be a radio operator. They told me it would help me get a good job when I got out."

He shook his head and laughed. "But I couldn't learn that stuff. It was too hard. So they put me in the infantry and sent me to 'Nam."

He turned to me then and peered into my face. It was almost dark and I was shivering. "It was like dying and going to hell," he said. "All my buddies ended up in them body bags. I lived. Just me. I came back home and they all thought I was lucky."

He stood up and began to hoist his bags. "Lucky, ain't I? Real lucky."

He took a few steps, then paused and glanced at me over his shoulder. "I don't need no friends," he mumbled. "Myself, that's all I need. Just me. Nobody else."

Overhead a gull shrieked, and the ducks quacked

from somewhere on the lake's dark surface. Shoving my hands into my pockets, I stood on the dock and watched Mr. Weems disappear into the night. I wanted to run after him, invite him to come home with me, have dinner, sleep in the guest room, but I didn't move or call out. I just let the distance between us grow and grow.

Chapter 10

As soon as Mr. Weems was out of sight, I walked through Town Centre, past Mister Charlie's and a row of offices where a few people worked late, past the movie theater and Branigan's restaurant, up the steps and across the pedestrian overpass. Ahead of me the mall rose, its glass roof glowing in the last light of the sun, but I turned away from it and the smells of Chinese food and fried chicken. I was going home.

Looking around me, I imagined the high-rise apartments and office buildings in ruins, the mall sacked, looted, burned, Adelphia a ghost town. No cars, no people, just a seagull or two crying on the wind.

Pulling my scarf tighter, I walked faster. Mr. Weems had talked to me all right, he'd given me a glimpse of his world, but right now, all by myself in the cold, I almost wished he hadn't.

When I finally opened my front door, it was after seven, and Mom met me in the hall.

"Kelly, where have you been?" She sounded so worried I felt guilty.

"At the library," I mumbled.

"You're supposed to be home before dark." Mom frowned at me. "If you'd called, I would have been happy to come and get you."

"I didn't have a quarter for the phone." I hung up my jacket and followed her to the kitchen. "Where's Dad?"

"Doing something with his computer." She handed me the silverware. "Here, set the table, Kelly, and I'll tell Greg dinner's ready."

*

"You were at the library again?" Dad helped himself to broccoli. The little oil lamps Mom used to illuminate the table made pinpoints of light in his eyes as he waited for me to answer.

"I told you I'm working on a paper for my global perspectives class.

"When is it due?"

"The first week in December, so I've got Thanksgiving vacation to work on it."

"Speaking of Thanksgiving," Mom said. "Is your mother definitely coming to dinner, Greg?"

"As far as I know." Dad helped himself to more chicken.

"And your brother?"

Dad shrugged. "As long as there's no charge, I'm sure Ralph will be here."

"Is he bringing Allison?" I poked at my chicken, trying to scrape the mushrooms off. If there were children more obnoxious than my cousin I hoped I'd never meet them.

"It depends on Jean," Dad said. "This might be her year to have Allison."

That was one good thing about divorce. Every other year Allison spent holidays with her mother, and I didn't have to see her.

"How about Aunt Eliza?" I asked Mom.

"She promised to be here." Mom smiled at me. Aunt Eliza, actually my great-aunt, was one of our favorite people. If she were coming, I could stand anybody, even Uncle Ralph and Allison, for a few hours.

Suddenly inspired with a wonderful idea, I looked at Mom and Dad. "How about inviting Mr. Weems to have Thanksgiving with us?"

"Absolutely not." Dad frowned at me over the rim of his wineglass.

I turned to Mom, knowing she was much more tender-hearted than Dad. "He won't have any place to go," I said. "The library will be closed and he'll be all alone and hungry. We always have more food than we can possibly eat."

But she shook her head, agreeing with Dad. "Honey, it's a family dinner," she said. "We can't have a stranger."

"Can you imagine how your grandmother would feel about Mr. Weems?" Dad asked me.

"It wouldn't bother Aunt Eliza," I said. "In fact, she'd be all for it."

"No, Kelly," Mom said, firming up her voice. "I'm sorry, but we can't have him here."

"He went to Vietnam and got all messed up and you don't even want to give him a meal?"

"Don't be so naive, Kelly." Dad said. "Do you see me using Vietnam as an excuse for everything I don't feel like doing?"

"You saw what he saw," I said. "Have you forgotten all about it? You must have killed people, seen your friends die. How do you live with it?" I could hear my voice rising, but I didn't care. "At least Mr. Weems hasn't turned into a money-making robot!"

"That's enough, Kelly!" Dad's voice rose too, and he leaned across the table, his finger jabbing at me. "I'm sick and tired of hearing about Vietnam and Mr. Weems. You know nothing about war. Nothing!"

I narrowed my eyes and scowled at him, hoping to convey wordlessly what I thought of his attitude. No matter what Dad said, I knew plenty about war. It killed people and hurt them, it ruined their lives, it took away their homes. You didn't actually have to be in a war to know how horrible it was.

"Just tell me one thing," I said. "Suppose I were a boy and there was a war in Central America or someplace. Would you want me to go? Would you want my body sent home in a plastic bag?"

"I won't play games with you, Kelly. We're not at

war, and you're not a boy." Without another word, Dad left the table.

I turned to Mom, expecting her support. "Who does he think he is, Rambo?"

Instead she looked angry. "He's right, Kelly. You shouldn't talk about things you don't know anything about. Especially Vietnam."

As she followed my father out of the room, I picked up my plate and carried it to the kitchen. Then I picked up Gandalf and retreated to my room. Shutting my door, I turned on the radio and tried to read the *Iliad*. I was almost finished; Hector and Achilles were about to meet on the battlefield, and I knew Hector was going to die.

I read one page, full of Achilles' glory, and then I tossed the book across the room. No matter what Mr. Hardy said, the *Iliad* was a war poem, full of horrible deaths, and I didn't want to read another word of it.

Opening my drawing tablet, I started a new picture. The lake at dusk, dark and murky, one seagull flying low over the water, and a girl walking alone, head down, her gray jacket merging with the color of the water.

*

A couple of days later, I went to the library. Although I was sure Mr. Weems would be glad to see me, he wouldn't even look at me, let alone speak to me. You'd think we'd never sat on the dock together feeding the ducks and talking about the end of the world.

To make matters worse, Julie and Keith were sitting

at a table on the other side of the room. They were holding hands, and Julie was whispering in his ear.

I slumped down in my chair and hid my face behind my book. I hadn't talked to Julie since she called me a junior freak, but it was pretty obvious she didn't miss me, not with Keith around.

Without raising my head, I glanced at them again just in time to see Keith kiss Julie. My heart beat a little faster and something swelled up in my throat, making it hard to swallow.

Blinking hard, I wiped my eyes quickly with the back of my hand. I certainly didn't want to kiss Keith or hold hands with him, but I hated to see him staring at Julie as if she were the only person in the world. Without looking at Mr. Weems or at Julie and Keith, I got up fast, grabbed my backpack, and slipped out the door.

As I was leaving the building, I saw Tim Andrews, the maintenance man, sweeping the foyer. I'd known him for ages, so I stopped to say hello. While we were talking, Mr. Weems sidled down the stairs, heading for the men's room. He had his bags with him, and a woman dodged aside, looking almost frightened.

"Poor old Bob," Tim said. "When we were in high school, I never thought he'd end up like this."

"That's Mr. Weems's first name — Bob?" I stared at Tim, trying to picture Mr. Weems — Bob Weems — in high school. Without the beard and the wild hair, without the garbage bags, just an ordinary teenager walking down the hall, getting his books out of his locker, sitting in class and listening to a teacher talk about poetry.

"What was he like?" I asked Tim. "When he was in school?"

"He was real quiet," Tim said, "the sort of person nobody notices much." He paused and looked at me. "Bob wasn't weird then. He didn't carry those sacks, and he didn't stink or anything, but he didn't have many friends. If he went to our class reunion, I bet nobody would remember his name."

I shifted my backpack and pictured a future Owen Mills class reunion. I could just hear Julie saying, "Kelly McAllister? Oh, yeah, that weird junior freak. I wonder whatever happened to her." Then she'd see Courtney or somebody and go running to meet her, giggling and shrieking and remembering all the fun she'd had in high school.

"He used to live on the old Steadman place," Tim went on. "His parents were tenant farmers. The house is long gone, so I guess he sleeps in that little strip of woods near the Seven-Eleven on Steadman Farm Way."

"Doesn't he have any family?"

"I don't know." Tim picked up a nickel somebody had dropped and put it in his pocket. He winked at me. "Fringe benefit."

"Don't you feel sorry for him?"

Tim shrugged. "He told me once he likes the way he lives."

"He told the social worker that too."

Tim swept a little pile of dirt and gravel and twigs into his dustpan. "Why are you so interested in him?" he asked without looking up from his task.

"I'm trying to interview him for a term paper. I'm writing about homeless people."

"Good luck. Getting Bob Weems to talk is just about as easy as getting a bent nail out of a piece of wood."

"Mrs. Hunter thinks going to Vietnam messed him up. What do you think?" I asked.

Tim shrugged. "Could be, I guess."

"Did you go there too?"

Tim paused and stared through the glass doors at the full parking lot and the bare trees. "I spent a year there when I was twenty," he said without looking at me. "One whole wasted year."

"What was it like?"

"I try not to think about it."

I waited, hoping Tim would say more, but he didn't even look at me again. While I stood there, he finished cleaning the foyer and went back into the library, leaving me to start walking home by myself.

*

"I saw Mr. Weems this morning," Mom said. She was sitting at her drawing table putting the finishing touches on a large dragon commissioned as a Christmas gift.

"Where?" I sipped my tea, breathing in the nice, warm steam rising from the cup.

"Coming out of the woods by the Seven-Eleven." She began shading the dragon's furled wings. "He looked so cold and lonely walking along with those heavy bags on his back."

"If you feel so sorry for him, why can't he come to Thanksgiving dinner?"

"Oh, Kelly, please don't start on that again." Mom swirled her brush in mauve watercolor. "I really feel bad about it, but we can't invite him to dinner."

Backing away from her, I said, "Well, if Mr. Weems can't come, maybe I won't come either. I'll go find where he lives in the woods and have my Thanksgiving dinner with him."

Mom laid her brush down and glared at me. "Don't you dare do something like that. Your Aunt Eliza is looking forward to seeing you and so are your grand-mother and Allison. I won't have you ruining dinner."

Leaning on her drawing table, I shoved my face close to hers, trying to get between her and her picture. "People are freezing and starving and dying in the real world," I told her, "and all you care about are drag-ons and unicorns and wizards. They aren't going to help anybody. The days of magic and sorcery are over, Mom!"

Without giving her a chance to say anything, I rushed on, too angry to stop. "You've always told me what a liberal you are, how you marched in those dem-onstrations and everything, but now you don't care about other people at all!" I was shouting at her and crying too. "How did you change so much?"

"Kelly, don't — " Mom stood up and her hand brushed a jar of water, toppling it onto the dragon.

As his colors fled across the paper, I turned and ran out of the room. Ignoring Mom's angry cry to come back, I thudded down the steps so fast I almost fell. What was wrong with her, with me, with everybody? Was the whole world going crazy? Or just me?

Chapter 11

AT DINNER, Mom was still angry about the dragon, but, even though I felt bad about it, I couldn't bring myself to apologize. After all, she spilled the water, not me. And, besides, if she hadn't been so against inviting Mr. Weems to Thanksgiving dinner, we wouldn't have quarreled and she wouldn't have ruined her painting.

Still, sitting there at the dinner table, listening to Mom and Dad talking, I wished Mom would forget about the whole thing. Having one parent hate me was enough.

While I was poking at my dessert, the phone rang. To my surprise, it was Julie inviting me to go to the library with her and Courtney.

"My Mom's driving, but she can't pick us up because she and Dad are playing indoor tennis," Julie told me. "and Courtney's Mom has aerobics class tonight." Julie was chewing gum hard, something she does when she's nervous, and I was sure she hadn't wanted to call me. Probably Courtney had talked her into it.

"So you're asking me in the hope my mother can drive us home, right?" I tried to sound really cool and detached.

"Don't be paranoid, Kelly." Julie laughed and chomped her gum so hard it sounded like a machine gun going off. "I haven't seen you for ages."

"And whose fault is that?" I asked.

"Oh, come on, Kelly," Julie giggled. "You know I didn't mean what I said, I was just in a bad mood or something." She paused, probably to blow a bubble. "I really want to see you."

"You're sure I won't bum you out or anything? I wouldn't want to ruin your night." I loaded my voice with sarcasm, and Julie giggled nervously.

"Oh, Kelly, I said I was sorry." Chomp, chomp, chompety chomp. "Can your mother pick us up or not?"

I could see Julie tossing her hair out of her face and shifting her weight from one hip to the other, hoping I'd just say yes and get it over with.

"I'll ask Mom, but right now she's kind of mad at me." Laying the receiver down, I poked my head into the dining room. "Can you drive Julie, Courtney, and me home from the library at nine? Mrs. Sinclair can drive us over, but she can't bring us back."

"What about Dianna?" Mom asked.

"She has aerobics class," I said.

Dad snorted, and I knew he was envisioning Courtney's mother, who's kind of overweight, leaping around in a leotard with a bunch of other fat ladies.

"I guess I can do it," Mom said, but her voice wasn't very friendly.

*

When we got out of Mrs. Sinclair's car, the wind hit us, and we ran into the library.

"You better not do anything to get us kicked out tonight," Courtney warned me. "I've got tons of research to do.

I shrugged and tagged along behind the two of them as they headed toward the women's room to comb their hair. Listening to them giggling about something Doug Walters had said to Courtney, I felt the gap widening between Julie and me. It used to be the two of us, laughing all the time about the same things. Now it was her and Courtney, and the stuff they laughed at seemed silly to me.

Frowning at my reflection in the mirror, I thought of something Georgia O'Keeffe had said about people; if only they were trees she'd like them better. Would I like Julie more if she were a maple or a willow? At least she wouldn't giggle or chew gum or talk about boys nonstop.

"Let's style Kelly's hair." Courtney suddenly lunged at me, holding her comb like a weapon.

As Julie watched, laughing as usual, I pulled away from Courtney. "I like my hair the way it is, thanks."

"But, Kelly, you'd look so cute if you'd fluff up your

bangs a little bit." Courtney tried to run her comb through my hair, but I dodged aside.

"Leave me alone," I said as a lady stepped out of a stall and frowned at us.

"I need to use the basin," she said to Julie who was hogging the mirror above it, combing and recombing her hair.

"Excuse *me*," Julie said sarcastically.

She and Courtney were convulsed with laughter as we left the lady to enjoy the basin all by herself, but I was embarrassed. They were acting like a pair of middle schoolers.

In the reference room, I saw Mr. Weems dozing over a book, but when I started to say hi, Julie grabbed my arm. "Don't you dare talk to that guy!" she hissed.

"For heaven's sake, Kelly, you are embarrassing me to death." Courtney pulled her notebook out of her backpack and glared at me. "Are you in love with him or something?"

Julie laughed as if that were the funniest thing she'd ever heard, but I wasn't amused. "I told you I have to interview him for my current issues paper."

I must have spoken louder than I thought because Mrs. Martin walked right up to us, singling me out for most of her attention but including Julie and Courtney. "You girls will have to sit down and work on something if you wish to remain in this room," she said. "Every time you come in here, you disturb other patrons, and I will not tolerate it."

We all sat down, but as Courtney opened her mouth

to defend herself, Mrs. Martin silenced her. "If I have to tell you to be quiet one more time," she said, "you'll be out the door. No warnings, no second chances. Is that clear?"

We nodded without looking at her. She was being grossly unfair, but she was in charge, not us. If I had to think of her as a tree it would be a spiny cactus, all dry and prickly, nothing I could like no matter how hard I tried.

"I hope you're satisfied," Courtney whispered to me.

I rolled my eyes and looked across the room at Mr. Weems. He was looking back through his little telescope, so I smiled and waved. He didn't respond, but Julie and Courtney did. They both scowled at me.

When Keith and Doug Walters walked into the reference room a few minutes later, both Julie and Courtney cheered up. For once, Courtney forgot to be a serious student, and Julie, who never had any scholarly pretentions, shut her math book and snuggled up next to Keith.

To get away from them, I went to the *Readers' Guide to Periodical Literature* and found a bunch of magazine articles on Vietnam veterans. From reading them, I discovered Mr. Weems had something called post-traumatic stress disorder. He wasn't alone either. One psychologist thought seventy-five percent of Vietnam veterans had it to some extent. It was treatable, he said, but not curable. About all the veterans could do was learn to cope with their memories.

Nothing could make them forget what they'd seen

and done, the articles said. The war was that horrible. Worse even than World War I in the poems I'd read. So some of the veterans took drugs and some of them drank, but I was sure Mr. Weems didn't do either. He sat in the library all day reading about the war and staring at photographs. Was he reliving it? Or just trying to figure out what had happened to him?

I looked up from my growing pile of note cards and saw him across the room, his head bent over a book. If only he'd talk to me again. According to what I was reading, he really needed help. The social worker had told him what to do, where to go, but he'd just waved him away.

Maybe the article I was reading would help him. At least he'd know he wasn't alone, he'd learn there were many, many men like him, men who — unlike my dad — couldn't put the war behind them and get on with their lives.

Getting up quietly, I walked across the room and paused by his table. "I found this article," I whispered as I laid the magazine down beside him. "You should read it."

Mr. Weems glanced at the article's title, "Help for Post-Traumatic Stress Disorder." Then he saw the photograph of two bearded veterans in army fatigues comforting each other. One was wearing a camouflage cap that said, "Vietnam — I was there and proud of it." The photographer had caught the man unaware. He had his hand to his mouth and he was crying. It hurt to look at the expression on his face.

"No." Mr. Weems pushed the magazine away and bent over the combat photos he was studying.

"But you can get help," I said, pointing at the part of the article describing therapy at veterans' hospitals. "See?" I shoved the magazine under his nose so he'd be sure to notice what I was talking about.

Mr. Weems looked up at me then, and the expression in his eyes scared me. He looked crazy, and I took a step backward as he jumped to his feet, yelling at me, his face red and angry.

"I told you I don't need no help, no friends, nothing!" he shouted. "Just leave me be, little girl. Leave me be, you hear me?"

I stared at him, too scared to move, and he threw the magazine at me. It bounced off my elbow, its pages fluttering, and landed at my feet. The whole room was silent as Mrs. Martin rose from her chair, one hand stretched toward Mr. Weems.

"Don't," she said, "don't."

But it was too late. Mr. Weems was gathering his bags, hoisting them to his shoulder, peering around the room like a trapped animal. "Leave me be," he shouted. "Can't I have no peace?" Then, bumping people with his bags, he hurried out of the room.

The minute Mr. Weems disappeared, everyone turned their attention to me, including Mrs. Martin.

Wishing I could disappear, I showed Mrs. Martin the magazine article. "I was trying to help him," I told her. "I wanted him to read this."

Ignoring the magazine, Mrs. Martin said, "Pack up your things and get out of here. If a trained social worker can't help that poor man, how on earth do you think you can?"

Turning away to hide my tears, I started jamming my books and papers into my backpack. Why wouldn't Mr. Weems trust me? Couldn't he see I really cared about him?

"And the rest of you." Mrs. Martin turned to Julie who was now sitting on Keith's lap, staring at me as if she didn't know whether to laugh or cry. "You can leave too. This is a library, not a circus!"

"That's just what we were about to do, Ma'am," Doug said in the sneering voice he uses with most adults. "Come on." He grabbed Courtney's arm and pulled her to her feet. "This place is a drag."

"Where are you going?" I asked as I followed them downstairs. I was so upset I could hardly get my feet to act right, and I had to hold onto the railing like an old lady. I was still crying too, but I kept my head down, hoping they wouldn't notice. I knew they were probably mad at me, especially Courtney, but they couldn't just go off and leave me. It was my mom who was driving them home.

Neither Julie nor Courtney looked at me, but Keith grabbed me around the waist and swung me in a circle while the people in line to check out books stared at us. "To the mall, Mad Dog — where else is there to go?" he said.

I squirmed away from him, uncomfortably aware of a funny tingling where he'd touched me. Not wanting him to guess how he made me feel, I put some distance between us and watched unhappily as he encircled Julie with his arm and hugged her close to him.

Trailing behind them, feeling invisible again, I looked down the path toward the lake. I thought I saw Mr. Weems hurrying away from us. I wanted to run after him and apologize, but I was scared of him now. He might yell at me again or even hit me.

Chapter 12

AT THE MALL, we all crowded into a booth at Friendly's. Keith treated me to the Reese's Pieces sundae he'd owed me since the first time I'd spoken to Mr. Weems, but I could barely taste the peanut butter sauce. All I could think about was Mr. Weems and how he'd shouted at me. There was a big lump of sadness in my throat and an ache in my chest, and I wished I were home in bed with Gandalf beside me.

"What's the matter, Mad Dog?" Keith stopped kissing Julie for a few seconds and stared at the melting glop in my dish. "Are you sick or something?"

"She must be," Courtney said, "causing a scene like that. What did you say to that maniac anyway?"

Julie giggled. "Maybe she propositioned him."

Courtney didn't even smile. She just rolled her eyes and sighed. "You and Mr. Weems would make the perfect couple, Kelly."

I straightened up then. "Don't you even care how sad he is?" I asked Courtney. "How would you like to live like that, all alone, no friends, no home, nothing at all?"

"Oh, please." Courtney scooped up the last of her banana split. "Spare me, Kelly."

"Are we supposed to go around crying over all the bums in the world?" Doug leaned across the table toward me. He was wearing his Owen Mills wrestling sweatshirt with a warm-up jacket over it, and his cheeks were still pink from the wind outside. "My dad says most of those guys live better than we do, with free handouts and shelters and no responsibilities."

"It's our tax dollars that support them," Courtney added, smiling at Doug.

"*Your* tax dollars?" I stared at Courtney.

"Our *parents*', then." She sipped her cola and watched me through narrowed eyes. "If you have to get technical."

"Doug, you don't really believe that sleeping in a shelter and eating at a soup kitchen is the good life, do you?" Keith wanted to know.

Doug shrugged his broad shoulders. "Hey," he said, "they don't have to go to work every day, do they?"

"They just worry about where their next drink is coming from," Julie put in.

"They're not all drunks." I leaned around Keith to see her, uncomfortably aware of my shoulder and arm pressing against his. "And even if they were, they still need help. Think how you'd feel if nobody cared whether you lived or died." I was getting close to crying again, so I raised my voice, forcing it to stay steady.

Julie looked at her ice cream dish and drew little lines in the leftover hot fudge with her spoon, but Courtney said, "Well, go ahead and be his friend. Share his cooties if that's what you want, but keep them to yourself, okay? And quit making a fool of yourself every time we go to the library!"

Doug made a kind of snorting sound, and Julie giggled, but Keith said, "It's almost nine o'clock. We better get back to the library to meet Kelly's mom.

After dumping the waitress's tip — thirty or forty pennies — in a glass of water, Doug followed the rest of us out of Friendly's. It seemed to me Courtney should have been a lot more embarrassed about that than about my scene with Mr. Weems, but she laughed and clung to Doug as if he were the cleverest person in Adelphia.

While we were waiting to cross Warfield Parkway, Keith grabbed my arm for a second. "They don't really mean half what they say, Mad Dog," he whispered. "Whatever their parents believe, they believe."

I nodded, but I wasn't sure that was an excuse. After all, my dad would certainly have agreed with Courtney and Doug, but I could see he was wrong.

"And anyway, Kelly, what you did was right," Keith went on. "You tried to help him."

"Come on, Keith." Julie grabbed Keith's hand and tugged him toward the street, hoping to take advantage of a break in the traffic.

I ran after them, dodging the cars. I still felt awful, but I was glad Keith didn't think I was totally weird. No matter what Julie and Courtney and Doug said, people like Mr. Weems needed somebody to care about them. Like whales and baby seals, they couldn't survive without help.

*

As we rode home, I saw Mr. Weems trudging ahead of us. He was walking on the road itself, ignoring the drivers swerving around him, blowing their horns and shouting at him.

"Hey, why don't you ask your mom to give your boyfriend a lift before somebody hits him?" Courtney leaned forward and hissed in my ear. "I'm sure we could squeeze him in. You could sit right next to him too, maybe even on his lap."

"Good grief," Mom said. "Doesn't that man realize he's on the road?"

As Mom left Mr. Weems behind, Courtney asked, "Do you think he should be allowed in the library, Mrs. McAllister?"

"Of course," Mom said. "The library's a public building. He has as much right to use it as anybody else, as long as he doesn't disturb anyone."

"But he does," Courtney said. "He stinks and pollutes the air everybody has to breathe, and tonight he yelled and threw a magazine at Kelly. He's really crazy."

"He what?" Mom stared at me and I slid down in my seat, mortified. Never had I disliked Courtney so much.

"It was my fault," I told Mom. "I thought I could help him, but I shouldn't have bothered him. It's no big deal, honest."

Mom raised her eyebrow, as Keith said, "Kelly showed him this magazine article. She just wanted to help him, but he kind of overreacted or something." He patted my shoulder. "She was pretty cool, I thought."

"You can tell me more about this later," Mom said to me as we pulled into Courtney's driveway.

Courtney and Doug got out together without even thanking Mom and ran up the sidewalk toward the front door.

"Who's next?" Mom asked. "You can drop Keith and me at my house," Julie said.

When the back seat was empty, I started fiddling with the radio, looking for some good music to fill in the short drive home. I didn't want to talk about Mr. Weems, so I turned the volume up and started singing along with an old song by the Talking Heads.

Right in the middle of the best part, Mom switched the radio off. "What happened in the library?" she asked.

"Like Keith said, I gave Mr. Weems a magazine and he threw it at me and left. It didn't hurt me or anything." I slumped lower in my seat and put my feet up on the dashboard. That stupid Courtney — why couldn't she have kept her mouth shut?

Mom turned to me. In the dim light from the instrument panel, I could see the worried expression on her face. "I know you want to help Mr. Weems, I understand that," she said slowly, "but I think you better stay away from him, sweetie. He sounds pretty unstable to me."

She reached out and tried to pull me against her side for a hug, but I tensed up. Was this something she thought she could make better with a kiss?

"I'm not your little baby anymore," I told her, "so just leave me alone."

We were in our own driveway now, and I opened the door and got out, shrugging off the hand she laid on my arm. Before she could say anything else, I ran into the house and up to my room. Scooping up Gandalf, who was sleeping peacefully on my bed, I buried my face in his fur and cried.

Everything in my whole life was wrong. Mr. Weems hated me, Mrs. Martin hated me, Julie and Courtney and Doug hated me. Even my own father hated me, and maybe my mother too. The only friend I had was Keith, but he was too much in love with Julie to be any real help.

Or was he? He'd been on my side in Friendly's, he'd understood what I'd tried to do, he'd even told Mom I'd been cool. Maybe he and Julie had a big fight after they got out of Mom's car, maybe he was coming home right now, totally fed up with Julie and her giggling and her chewing gum.

Wiping my eyes on my sleeve, I went to my window and looked across the street at Keith's house. The front porch light shone on his driveway and cast a criss-cross shadow from his basketball net across the front of the garage, but his bedroom windows were dark. While I watched, his father came outside and set a garbage can by the curb for tomorrow's pickup. Then, as usual, he jogged off down Peter Pan Way, moving almost as lightly as Keith.

I sighed as Mr. Myers disappeared into the blackness beyond the streetlight. Keith was probably sitting on Julie's couch right this minute, making out with her. For all I knew they were both laughing at me for being so dumb. It was silly to think anything else.

Anyway, it was Mr. Weems I should be worrying about, not Keith. A gust of wind rattled the branches outside my window, and I shivered. He shouldn't have gotten so mad at me. All I wanted to do was help him and be his friend. You'd think he'd be grateful.

*

Much later, when I'd gotten into bed, I heard Mom tap on my door. "Kelly, are you asleep?"

"No." I watched her walk to my bed. When she sat down beside me, I threw my arms around her and hugged her hard. "I'm sorry about your dragon and the things I said," I whispered. "I didn't mean it."

Mom stroked my hair the way she used to when I was little. "Are you sure you're okay?" she asked.

"What do you mean?" I felt myself get tense all over.

"I don't know." She ran a finger lightly down my nose. "You seem so unhappy." Her voice trailed off, as if she couldn't find the right words for what she wanted to say.

I lay still for a moment, watching the shadows shift on my ceiling. "Do you think I'm weird, Mom?"

"Of course not." Mom sounded absolutely positive, and I knew I'd asked the wrong question. No mother ever thinks her child is weird. Even Mrs. Weems, if she were still alive, probably thought her son was just going through a stage. Any day, she'd tell herself, he'd cut his hair, clean himself up, and get a nice job in a bank.

"Well, sometimes I think I'm weird," I went on. "People like Julie and Courtney, they seem made for Adelphia, but me — I don't know where I belong." I clung to her hand, not wanting to tell her how scared I was. "Did you ever feel like that when you were my age?"

Mom nodded. "Lots of times. In fact, I still do." She bent closer and her hair tumbled down and tickled my nose. "How many women my age spend their time drawing dragons and unicorns?"

"But doesn't that scare you a little bit?"

"Sure." Mom gave me a big hug. "Everybody feels scared sometimes. Even Julie and Courtney. We all have a secret self we keep hidden because we're afraid of what other people might think."

After Mom kissed me good night, I tried to imagine

Courtney and Julie worrying about themselves or being scared, but they were too pretty, too popular to have the kind of dark, secret self I felt growing in me. They fit in with all the other girls I saw laughing at the mall and the lake and the pool and the skating rink.

No matter what Mom said, I was the one who didn't belong, the odd one, the weird one. Like Mr. Weems, I'd never have any friends, I'd never fit in, nobody in my class would remember my name.

Chapter 13

THE NEXT COUPLE of days rushed by, full of over-
due assignments and tests. I knew I should apologize to Mr. Weems for upsetting him, but I didn't have
a chance to go near the library. In a way, I was kind of
relieved because I wasn't sure I had the courage to face
him now.

I didn't see Julie or Courtney except in school, and
then we passed each other like strangers. I played basketball a few times with Keith, but he spent most of
his time with Julie. The Wednesday before Thanksgiving, I was glad to leave school behind for four days.
No more Julie and Courtney, no more Mr. Poland, no
more having to act like I enjoyed walking to my classes
by myself.

*

When I woke up Thanksgiving morning, the first
thing I saw was a gray sky and falling rain. Gandalf was

curled into a ball, purring in my ear, and I stroked his fur, glad for his company. Usually I loved to wake up to the smell of roasting turkey, but this morning it reminded me of Mr. Weems.

Here I was looking forward to eating a delicious dinner while he wandered the streets of Adelphia, wet and cold and miserable. He had no library to go to, no turkey to eat, no friends to visit. To Mr. Weems, Thanksgiving was just another day, worse than most because the library was closed.

"Kelly?" Dad stuck his head into my room, startling me. "It's after eleven, our guests are due at one, and your mother could use your help."

I turned my head and looked at him. He was wearing the gray sweater vest I'd given him last year for Christmas, darker gray corduroy slacks, a blue button-down shirt, and a paisley tie.

"Tell her I'll be down as soon as I take my shower," I said.

"Put on something nice, Kelly. Your grandmother hasn't seen you for months," Dad said. "And clean up your room. I don't see how any self-respecting person can live in such squalor."

I could have reminded him of the apartment he once lived in, the one with the socks on the radiator and the dirty dishes in the sink and the cockroaches as big as rats, but I wasn't up to starting a scene. Instead, I stumbled down the hall to the bathroom, feeling as if I hadn't slept nearly as long as I would have liked to.

After I washed my hair, I contemplated using

mousse to make it stand up in spikes but decided against it. Dad would just make me rinse it out.

After surveying my closet, I pulled on an old lace-collared blouse I'd found at Value Village, a pair of black tights, my favorite black granny boots, and dropped my jumper over everything. It was my best outfit, and if Grandmother didn't like it, too bad.

Downstairs, Mom was hard at work preparing sweet potatoes. In blue jeans and an old University of Maryland sweatshirt, she was still dressed to cook, not to eat.

"You look very nice, Kelly," she said as she jammed the potatoes into the food processor. "Please put on an apron and make the salad. There's lettuce, tomatoes, cucumbers, mushrooms, zucchini, and stuff in the crisper."

While I was tying the apron, Dad came in for a cup of coffee. "Don't you have any other shoes?" he asked me.

"What's wrong with these?"

"They look like combat boots."

"Oh, Greg," Mom sighed. "All the kids wear those things."

"If they all wore their socks on their ears would you want your daughter doing it too?"

Mom laughed and gave Dad a kiss. "Don't be silly."

Shaking his head, Dad poured a cup of coffee and retreated again to his den where he was, as usual, doing something boring with his computer. Balancing the budget, perhaps, or crunching a few numbers, as he put it.

"Why is he always so critical?" I asked Mom. "Can't he ever say anything nice to me?"

Mom gave me a hug. "He's a little tense, honey. He always is when his mother visits."

"Don't blame it on Grandmother. He puts me down all the time, and you know it. Sometimes I think he hates me."

"Oh, Kelly, try not to be so sensitive. Your father loves you very much." From the look she gave me as she said this, I knew she didn't want me to get started on the great attorney's defects.

Since it was Thanksgiving, I just muttered, "Well, he sure doesn't act like it."

While Mom ran upstairs to change her clothes, I went back to chopping things for the salad. Whack, whack, whack went the knife, and little pieces of celery flew everywhere. Poor Gandalf got all excited, hoping it was turkey, but after one sniff, he stalked away, obviously disappointed.

✳

At one o'clock, the doorbell rang, and Uncle Ralph, Allison, and Grandmother hurried into the house, anxious to escape the rain and wind. There was a flurry of hugging and laughing and conversation, but in less than five minutes we were sitting in the living room staring at each other as if we were strangers waiting in an airport for the next plane out.

When Dad appeared with a tray of drinks, things got a little better, and people began real conversations.

"Where's Eliza?" Grandmother asked Mom. "I thought she was coming."

Mom glanced at her watch. "She should be here any minute. When the weather's bad, her arthritis slows her down."

Grandmother made a little face and shook her head. "Too bad she has arthritis. Quite a few of the ladies at Morningside House need walkers to get around. It's so depressing." She patted her blue curls, held stiffly in place with hairspray, and then smoothed her skirt over her knees.

When no one said anything, Grandmother went on, "Eliza should give up that place of hers. It's foolish for someone her age to live alone when she could have a nice little apartment like mine. Three meals a day and things happening all the time. Bridge tournaments, shopping trips to the mall, outings to dinner theaters and museums. Why, she could even take yoga or painting classes — she used to be rather artistic, didn't she?"

While Grandmother continued to extol the virtues of living in a retirement community, I turned my attention to Allison. She was wearing a stylish outfit I'd seen in the Hitching Post and a tiny bit of blusher and eye shadow which made her look pretty sophisticated for a ten year old. Pretty dumb too, if you ask me, and I couldn't help thinking she should have been Julie's cousin, not mine.

"So, Allison," I said, "how's school?"

She sighed. "Boring."

I nodded. "Mine too."

"But you go to Owen Mills," she said. "If I was in high school, I'd never be bored."

"Why not? What's so special about high school?"

Allison giggled and rolled her eyes at the adults, indicating they weren't supposed to hear what she was about to say. "Well, you can go to games and parties and have boyfriends and ride around in cars," she whispered.

"Big deal." I almost felt sorry for Allison. She didn't know anything, poor kid. I glanced at her, thinking I should give her some real insights into high school life, but she was staring at me as if I were the one who didn't know beans.

"When I'm a teenager, I'm going to parties every night," she said with complete conviction.

"Here comes Aunt Eliza," Dad interrupted us.

"Talk to her about Morningside House," Grandmother prompted Mom as she got up to go to the door. "What would happen if she had a heart attack living on that farm all by herself?"

I was happy to see Aunt Eliza burst in, shaking her umbrella and laughing at something Mom said. After giving her a hug and a kiss, she turned to me.

"Kelly," she cried, squeezing me speechless. "You look adorable!"

Then, brushing aside Dad's offer to lend a hand, she crossed the room and sank into our old Boston rocker. I watched her sip a glass of wine as she talked to Mom.

Although she was almost eighty, older than Grandmother by at least ten years, she seemed to have much more energy and vitality; in some ways she was more alive than I was. Her eyes sparkled, her features shifted with each change of expression, and her voice rose and fell as she hopped from one subject to another, daring everyone to keep up with her.

By the time we were seated at the table, she had talked about the books she'd read recently, her plans for next year's garden, and was just beginning to describe her volunteer work at the soup kitchen.

"That doesn't sound very safe, Eliza." Grandmother watched her spoon a mound of mashed potatoes onto her plate. "All those drunks and drug addicts coming in for a free meal. Aren't you frightened?"

"Just because a man has no home and no job doesn't mean he's dangerous," Aunt Eliza said.

"Mom's right," Uncle Ralph agreed with Grandmother. "Stay out of downtown Baltimore. Do what Mom does — shop at Harbor Place where everything's clean and nice. Don't go looking for trouble."

"Someone needs to help," Aunt Eliza insisted.

"People are getting too soft," Uncle Ralph said. "They expect the world on a silver platter."

As Uncle Ralph bent his head over his plate, I turned to Aunt Eliza. "There's this man in Adelphia," I told her. "He doesn't have a home or a job or anything. He just walks around with these big bags or sits in the library reading."

"Oh, Kelly," Dad said, "can't you ever talk about anything else? I'm sure no one wants to hear about Mr. Weems."

Ignoring him, I spoke directly to Aunt Eliza. She'd be interested in Mr. Weems, I knew she would. And she'd care too. "He's a Vietnam vet, that's what's wrong with him," I explained, "but when I wanted to invite him here for Thanksgiving, they wouldn't let me."

"If you saw this man, Eliza, you'd understand," Dad said. "He's a vagrant, filthy, crawling with lice and God knows what else." He spread his hands and shook his head. "Kelly's going through some kind of altruistic stage, I think."

While Dad and Uncle Ralph shared a laugh at my expense, Grandmother stared at me, shocked. "Your parents couldn't invite someone like that into their home, Kelly."

"Oooh," Allison sucked in her breath. "I know who Kelly means. I've seen him and he's horrible. My mother keeps telling the librarians they should kick him out before he goes crazy and does something awful."

"Don't be so stupid, Allison! He's just a sad, home-less person, and he'd never hurt anybody." Glancing at Mom, I prayed she wouldn't mention the magazine incident, but she was too busy passing the cranberry sauce to Uncle Ralph to say anything.

"Kelly, don't use that tone of voice at the dinner

table." Dad frowned at me. "This Weems business has gone far enough."

"My mother won't even let me stay at the library if he's there," Allison told Grandmother primly.

"For your information, he has post-traumatic stress disorder," I told Allison, "and you should have a little sympathy for him."

Allison stared at me, her fork halfway to her mouth. "You're weird," she mouthed at me.

I gave her my best withering look. Since when did a kid like Allison have the right to call me weird? What did she know about anything? While I watched, she made a face at me and then started forking mashed potatoes into her mouth.

As I passed a basket of rolls to Grandmother, I glanced at the people sitting around our table, their faces softened by candlelight. Was Aunt Eliza the only one who *didn't* think I was weird?

"Post-traumatic stress disorder is just another fancy word," Uncle Ralph said, bringing Mr. Weems back into the conversation. "The only vets anybody cares about are the screw-ups using Vietnam as an excuse. Let's face it, they'd be bums whether there was a war or not."

"Can't we talk about something else?" Mom asked as she passed the broccoli to Uncle Ralph.

Grandmother nodded. "I'm sick to death of people talking about Vietnam after all these years. Remember what your father used to say?"

She turned to Dad and Uncle Ralph and then focused on me. "He thought we should do the job right and drop a few atomic bombs. If it hadn't been for those hippies lying down in the streets and making fools of themselves, we would have won that war."

"Well, thank God for the hippies then," Aunt Eliza said.

"Would someone like seconds?" Mom's voice was a little louder than necessary, but she was still trying to smile.

"Pass some cranberries my way," Dad said. "We don't want to miss the big game, do we?"

Like magic, the conversation veered away from Vietnam to football, but after dinner, while Mom, Aunt Eliza, and I cleaned up, I asked Aunt Eliza about the soup kitchen.

"It's run by a Quaker group," she told me, "down on Preston Street, and we get all kinds of folks, everybody from old alcoholics to young families." She handed me a bowl to rinse. "Do you have anything like that in Adelphia?"

I shook my head. "Except for Mr. Weems, I don't think anybody around here needs free food."

"Where does he get his meals then?"

"From dumpsters, he says."

"And where does he sleep?"

"Somebody told me he used to live in a tenant house on the old Steadman farm, and they think he camps out in the woods where his house was." As I jammed a handful of silverware into the dishwasher, I glanced out the window; rain streamed down the glass, and the bare trees shivered in the wind. It pained me to picture Mr. Weems trudging along a highway or camped out in the woods somewhere, cold and wet and hungry.

"I hope he had a good meal somewhere," Mom said.

"He could have had one here," I reminded her.

She sighed and shook her head. "You heard your grandmother, Kelly," she said. "You know how she feels."

"Well, she and Allison and Uncle Ralph could have eaten at King's Contrivance or someplace fancy like that, where even the dishwashers probably have college educations. I sure wouldn't have missed them."

"Kelly, Kelly, Kelly." Aunt Eliza gave me a strong hug. "She's your father's mother."

"He could've gone with them." I pulled away, feeling sulky. "He's just as bad as they are."

"He used to be such an idealist," Mom said, sticking up for Dad as usual. "In fact, when he started law school he was going to be a public defender and work for the poor."

"So what happened?" I asked.

"I truly don't know, Kelly. Somehow he just ended up in corporate law." She turned away and busied herself scraping the roasting pan. From the way she acted, you would have thought my father had nothing to do with the way his life turned out; he started in one direction, then changed completely, as if he were a character in a bad writer's novel.

"Then he wasn't sincere," I said, realizing my voice was rising. "He didn't really care about people, just money. That's why he's in corporate law. He didn't just end up there — he chose it!"

"Maybe we should pack up a nice selection of leftovers and go look for your Mr. Weems, Kelly," Aunt Eliza interrupted while I was pausing to take a breath. "What do you think?"

"That's a great idea. I'd love to get out of here for a while." I glanced at Mom, but she was busy measuring coffee into the pot.

"Take whatever you think he'd like. We have plenty," Mom said.

As I searched for paper plates, I hoped Aunt Eliza and I were doing the right thing. She didn't know about the scene in the library or the food Mr. Weems had thrown in the trash can. If he yelled at me again or hurled the food in my face, what would Aunt Eliza think?

Chapter 14

"HERE, KELLY, let me help." Mom pushed me aside gently and found the plates. Then the three of us piled them high with food and covered them with plastic wrap. Hoping for the best, I grabbed my jacket, and followed Aunt Eliza down the hall.

As we passed the living room, Grandmother looked up from the Scrabble game she and Allison were playing. "Are you leaving already, Eliza?"

"No, no," Aunt Eliza said. "Kelly and I are going out on an errand. We'll be back soon.

Outside, the rain hit us in the face, hard and cold as ice pellets, and we hurried to the shelter of Aunt Eliza's pickup truck. She lives on a small farm west of Adelphia and insists she needs a four-wheel drive vehicle to get up her driveway in the winter. And it might as well be a truck, she told Dad, because she has to haul stuff sometimes. Boards, fertilizer, plants, stones, bricks — who knows what.

Following my directions, Aunt Eliza headed down Warfield Parkway. It was almost dark now, and the rain made it hard to see, but I was sure I'd spot Mr. Weems trudging along ahead of us. We drove for miles, looping all over Adelphia, cruising up and down Route 29, even going as far as I–95, but there wasn't a sign of him. Finally I told Aunt Eliza to try the 7-Eleven on Steadman Farm Way. Maybe we'd see him there, I thought, not far from the woods he called home.

"I could use a cup of coffee," Aunt Eliza said as we pulled into the crowded parking lot. "How about you?"

While she waited in the truck, I ran inside, elbowing my way to the coffee pots. You sure could tell the 7-Eleven was the only place open in Adelphia. I fixed Aunt Eliza's coffee black, but I poured at least six half-and-halfs in mine, making it a nice shade of golden tan, and added sugar too. It's not the coffee itself I like but the things you add to it.

As I was paying the girl at the cash register, I heard the man behind me say. "There's that bum again."

Grabbing my change, I hurried outside. Mr. Weems was poking in the trash can beside the door.

I stopped a few feet away, afraid he might yell at me. "Hi, Mr. Weems," I said, but my voice sounded phony even to me, like someone in a play feigning surprise.

He tensed a little, then backed away from the trash can as if I'd caught him in a shameful act. He nodded, but he didn't look at me as he gathered his bags.

"I'm sorry I bothered you the other night," I said.

"You know, at the library. I just thought, well, that article, I thought you might want to.... " My voice trailed off, and I shrugged, too nervous to look him in the face.

The silence between us grew and stretched, but at least Mr. Weems didn't turn away. Instead, he lingered beside the trash can. When I dared to catch his eye, he shifted his gaze past me and stared at the woods bordering the parking lot.

"Would you like some coffee?" I held out the cups, hoping he wouldn't hurl them back in my face. "This one's black, the other's got cream and sugar. They're nice and hot, just right for a rainy night."

I watched steam curl up from the cups, but Mr. Weems didn't take one. Instead he shook his head and took a few steps backward toward the trees.

"Don't go," I said. Aunt Eliza was getting out of the truck, carefully balancing the plates of food. As she approached us, Mr. Weems continued to edge away, his face almost invisible under the dripping rim of Dad's ski cap.

"We brought you Thanksgiving dinner," I said, following him, still holding out the cups. "It's not hot anymore, but it's still good. I made the cranberries myself and my mom did the rest. Turkey and stuffing and mashed potatoes and broccoli with cheese sauce. Rolls, too, and sauerkraut and carrots. Pumpkin pie for dessert."

I paused for breath. By now, the rain was working

its way down the back of my neck, creeping in between my skin and the collar of my army jacket. Water was soaking through the soles of my shoes, and my fingers were freezing. How did Mr. Weems stand being outside in weather like this, night after night?

I watched him linger on the edge of the dark, wet woods. Just as I thought he was going to lose himself in the trees, he stopped and stood still, his head bowed. Slowly Aunt Eliza drew near, holding the plates like an offering. Little drops of water sparkled all over the plastic wrap, catching the light from the store.

Aunt Eliza smiled at him, and for the first time I realized I was taller than she was. When had that happened? To Mr. Weems, Aunt Eliza must have seemed tiny, frail, white-haired, no one to fear. "Please," she said as kindly as a fairy godmother. "Take the food."

Shifting his bags to one hand, Mr. Weems took the plates from Aunt Eliza. While I held my breath, he backed away again, putting space between us, as wary as a stray dog I'd once seen dragging garbage out of our trash can.

"This is my great-aunt Eliza," I told Mr. Weems.

He nodded and a bead of rain water ran down his nose and dripped off the end.

"Would you like to sit in the truck with us while you eat?" Aunt Eliza asked. "It's a terrible night."

He stared at her as if she had used words he had forgotten the meaning of. Then he shook his head.

Mumbling something neither of us could understand, he walked away from us, struggling to balance the plates and his bags.

"He didn't take the coffee," I said as he vanished into the dark woods. My knees were weak with relief. Maybe he hadn't thanked us, maybe he hadn't gotten into the truck, but he hadn't yelled and he hadn't thrown anything and, most important of all, he'd accepted the food.

Aunt Eliza climbed into the truck and I sat down beside her, warming my hands on the cup before prying the lid off. We sipped our coffee slowly, our breath steaming the windshield, blurring the people coming and going from the 7-Eleven.

"So that was your Mr. Weems," Aunt Eliza said.

"I've tried and tried to be his friend, but he won't let me," I said. After hesitating a moment, I got up my courage and told her the rest. "Last week, he yelled at me in the library when I showed him a magazine article about post-traumatic stress disorder. Why won't he let me help him?" Tears swam up in my eyes, and I tried to brush them away with my sleeve before Aunt Eliza noticed.

She drew me close, and squeezed me against her bony side. "I know it's hard, Kelly, but some people don't trust anybody. They won't let you near them, no matter how much you care about them."

"But he could die of pneumonia this winter. Or starve to death," I sobbed. "Can't somebody put him in a hospital and make him better?"

"If he's been in the army, he could get treatment in a V.A. hospital, but he has to go there himself. No one will come looking for him, Kelly. Not unless he breaks a law."

"But vagrancy is illegal. He could be put in jail for that, and then they could get him to a hospital."

"You haven't spent much time in a city, have you?" Aunt Eliza took a sip of coffee. "Let me tell you, Kelly, there are hundreds, thousands maybe, of homeless people in every city in this country, and nobody is arresting them. Do you know why? There's no place to put them all."

"That's awful." I slumped down in the seat and watched the rain sluice down the windshield. "Look at all the money some people have, more than most of them know what to do with, my parents included. It's not fair that other people don't even have a house or a job or anything."

"Oh, Kelly, I agree with you completely." Aunt Eliza patted my hand. "But I'm afraid life never has been fair."

I slid further down in the seat, disappointed in the way she was talking. It reminded me of arguing with my dad. Like him, Aunt Eliza seemed to know all the answers.

"That's no excuse," I mumbled. "Saying life's not fair. It never will be if people don't do anything to change it. The rich people will just keep getting richer and richer."

"That's why I work in the soup kitchen, Kelly," Aunt

Eliza said. "I know it's not much, but at least it keeps a few people from starving."

"Well, when I get older, I'm going to do something about it. "

"Like what?" Aunt Eliza asked, as she started the engine and backed out of the parking lot.

"If they still have the Peace Corps or Vista, I'll join up. My mother was going to do that, but she married my father instead. I'm not going to be like her and sit around drawing dragons all day."

Aunt Eliza gave me a quick look, then returned her concentration to the wet road ahead. "I can think of lots of worse ways she could spend her time, Kelly. Aren't you being a little hard on her?"

"Well, she shouldn't have copped out. She could have been a real artist, you know, or a political activist; she could have done something worthwhile with her life. She just gave up, that's all. She took the easy way."

Aunt Eliza shook her head. "You don't think being your mother is worthwhile?"

I watched the windshield wipers flap back and forth, back and forth. How could anybody answer a question like that?

"People change, Kelly," Aunt Eliza went on. "Life rubs off their rough edges, they learn to settle for less, to be less."

"Not everybody," I said. "Look at Georgia O'Keeffe. She never drew anything little and silly."

"She had more strength than most people. That's what made her a great artist. Just because your mother couldn't be Georgia O'Keeffe doesn't mean she's a failure as a human being."

I thought of Mom sitting at her drawing table, listening to one of her old albums, painting her dragons and unicorns and wizards. Sure, it was better than going to aerobics or shopping at the mall — but was it enough? Maybe for her, but not for me.

Turning to Aunt Eliza, I said, "I'm not going to let life wear me down. I'll never settle for less. Never!" But even as I spoke, I was scared, because how did I know what life was going to do to me? I was only fourteen years old, and my future was as dark as the rainy night we were driving through.

Aunt Eliza smiled and slapped me on the knee. "Good for you, Kelly," she said. "But in the meantime, why don't you come to the soup kitchen with me? We could use some young blood."

"I'd love to," I told her. For the first time all day, I felt myself relax. Aunt Eliza hadn't laughed at me or told me I was too young to know anything. Instead of saying, "Tell me about it when you're forty," she'd said, "Good for you," and her voice had pride in it, not scorn.

*

The next three days, my Thanksgiving vacation, crept past full of rain and bad weather and nothing to do but read and draw and hang around Mom's studio, listening to her old Simon and Garfunkel albums and feeling more and more depressed.

"These songs are so sad," I said one afternoon.

"Sometimes I see you stop painting and just sit there staring out the window, singing along with them. Maybe you should play the Stones or the Beatles or some of the others."

I ran a finger along the spines of her albums, Bob Dylan, The Moody Blues, Cat Stevens, Credence Clearwater Revival, Crosby, Stills and Nash, the Beatles, Gordon Lightfoot, Joni Mitchell, Judy Collins, Joan Baez — she had them all.

Mom didn't answer. She just sighed and bent closer to the unicorn she was painting, concentrating on the tree trunks in the background of the picture. Her pen moved deftly over the watercolor, delicately cross-hatching the texture of bark. Simon and Garfunkel were singing softly about a guy on a bus with his girl friend Cathy, "counting the cars on the New Jersey Turnpike." Just like him they'd all gone to look for America, but you knew they weren't going to find it, nobody was, it was gone like a dream, it didn't exist except in your imagination.

"Remember that graffiti we saw the last time we took the Metro into Washington?" I asked her. "'The American Dream is the world's nightmare.' Do you think that's true?"

Mom looked up from her tiny forest in fairyland. "Oh, Kelly, I don't know. Let's have a cup of tea before we get totally depressed." Flipping off the record player, she ran down the stairs ahead of me, her hair floating behind her like a kid's.

"You're as bad as Julie," I told her as she set matching mugs on the kitchen counter and filled the tea kettle. "You don't want to talk about anything that might depress you."

Before she could answer, Dad joined us, and tea expanded into leftover turkey sandwiches and cranberry sauce, followed by the last of the pumpkin pie.

While we were having a second cup of tea, Dad turned to me. "Have you finished that report you were working on?"

I shrugged, not wanting to tell him it was nothing more than a jumble of notes about post-traumatic stress disorder, the plight of the homeless, and the Vietnam War. I still didn't have a clear focus because I didn't understand the war very well. Or what happened afterward. Especially to people like Mr. Weems.

"It's almost done," I mumbled because Dad was sitting across the counter from me, obviously waiting for an answer.

"Do you need to go to the library? I have to use their copy machine and do a little research, so I can drive you over there." He swallowed the last of his tea and stood up, checking me over as he did so. "Hurry up and change," he said.

"Change?" I stood up too and stared at him. "My clothes? Or myself?"

"You know what I mean, Kelly. Your pants have a hole in the knee and your sweatshirt has paint all over it." Nudging Gandalf out of his way with his foot, he rinsed his mug and put it in the dishwasher.

"You should pay more attention to your appearance," he went on while his back was turned. "Even your grandmother noticed your sloppiness on Thanksgiving."

"I suppose she thinks I should buy my clothes at the Hitching Post like Allison." I scooped up Gandalf and buried my face in his soft gray fur. "And smear mauve blusher all over my cheeks."

"All you need to do is ask, Kelly," Dad said. "I'd be happy to give you a clothing allowance."

"Oh, Greg." Mom slung an arm around my shoulders, "Kelly's an artist, not a clotheshorse. You should be proud of her."

The great attorney cast his eyes skyward as if he were longing for insight — what could he find in me to be proud of? "I don't want her to be a clotheshorse," he said, his voice straining for patience. "I simply want her to look neat and well-groomed. And don't tell me that's out of date — I see plenty of girls her age, her friends included, wearing clothes without holes in colors other than black. Clothes that actually *fit*."

"Look, Dad," I said, "I really need to get to the library, so can't we just go? I'll pretend I'm not your daughter, just some strange girl you never saw before, okay?"

Dad sighed and went to the closet for his coat. As I slipped into his old army jacket, he shook his head. "Don't you have something else? I seem to remember a nice pink ski parka."

"Too small." I slung my backpack over one shoulder and kissed Mom good-bye. "Remember, play the Beatles, their early stuff — 'I Want to Hold Your Hand' or something. Nothing heavy like 'Imagination.'"

She shook her head. "I haven't been able to listen to the Beatles since John was murdered," she said. "How about the Stones instead?"

I told her they'd be okay, and then Dad and I were running through the rain to the car. He tuned the radio to his favorite news station and all the way to the library we listened to a rundown of the latest wars in the Mideast. Very cheerful.

Chapter 15

TRUE TO MY WORD, I left Dad at the copy machine as if he were a stranger and ran upstairs to the reference room, hoping to see Mr. Weems. But he wasn't sitting at his table. Instead a mother was occupying his chair helping a sulky, bored girl do her homework.

I hung around for a while, looking up a few more magazine articles on the homeless, but Mr. Weems didn't appear. Finally I decided to use the rest of my time visiting Mrs. Hunter.

I found her in a corner of the children's room setting up a Christmas display. She gave me a hug and let me help her arrange the picture books.

"We're not very busy today," she said. "The Sunday after Thanksgiving — I guess everybody's at the mall starting their Christmas shopping."

"I didn't see Mr. Weems upstairs," I said, "but I can't imagine *him* at the mall."

"You didn't hear about him?" Mrs. Hunter asked.

I stared at her. "Hear what?"

She sighed and tidied a row of books. "You know how many complaints we were receiving about him. Well, our director decided we had to do something."

"What did you do?" I clutched my notes and stared at her. The expression on her face made my heart beat a little faster, and I tensed up, bracing myself for bad news.

"It was Mrs. Martin's idea actually. She told Mr. Weems she had no objection to his using the library. After all, it's a public place." Mrs. Hunter bent her head over one of the picture books as if she were ashamed to look at me. "Then she said he couldn't bring his bags inside. They took up too much space and created a hazard, you know, blocking the aisles. And, besides, they had an offensive odor."

"But his whole life is in those bags. Everything he owns! He never puts them down unless they're right next to him!"

"I know," Mrs. Hunter said sadly. "Believe me, Kelly, Mrs. Martin feels terrible about the whole thing."

"So he hasn't come back? Is that it?"

"She talked to him last week, and we haven't seen him since." Mrs. Hunter put the last book on the shelf, a beautifully illustrated nativity story open to a picture of the poor shepherds admiring the baby Jesus.

"That's awful." I glared at Mrs. Hunter, trying to

remember it wasn't her fault. "Just because a few narrow-minded, selfish people complained about a poor homeless person he gets kicked out of the only place where he could stay warm and dry! I hate those people, I hate them!"

"It's very sad," she agreed. "Especially at this time of year."

"Can we check these books out?" A little girl wedged herself in between Mrs. Hunter and me and pointed at the row of Christmas books. "I want the one about the little boy with the drum."

As Mrs. Hunter handed the girl her book, I wandered back upstairs. Mrs. Martin was sitting at the information desk, reading *Publishers Weekly*. She didn't look pleased when she saw me standing in front of her. "Can I help you find a book?" she asked.

"Mrs. Hunter told me what you said to Mr. Weems," I said, "and I just want to tell you what an awful thing you did." My heart was pounding so hard I felt like putting my hand over it to keep it in my chest, and my voice had to squeeze past a big lump in my throat, but I was determined to let her know what I thought.

Mrs. Martin stood up then and said, "Why don't you come into my office for a minute?"

Even though I was scared, I followed her in there. After all, she wasn't the principal or even one of my teachers. What could she do to me?

"Sit down." Mrs. Martin took a seat behind her desk, and I sat opposite her, staring at the potted plant, the clean blotter, the neat stack of books, the photograph of two little girls (her daughters?), the coffee mug full of pencils and pens.

Mrs. Martin leaned toward me. "I think you should know something, Kelly, before you begin criticizing a decision that was very difficult for me to make."

I slumped in the uncomfortable chair, avoiding her eyes. What was she going to say to justify herself? "You gave in to a bunch of middle-class taxpayers," I said, trying to sound tough.

"There was more to it than that." Mrs. Martin paused and steepled her fingers, stared at them intently for a few seconds, then looked at me again. "Do you remember the night you provoked Mr. Weems into yelling and throwing a magazine at you?"

"I didn't provoke him." I swallowed hard, not liking the way she was twisting things. "I told you then I was trying to help him."

"And I told you to leave him alone. Not for the first time either." She sighed. "That incident had repercussions, Kelly. Several patrons felt his outburst was proof Mr. Weems was a dangerous person. As a result, the director felt he had to end Mr. Weems's visits to the library."

The office was very still then. The only sound was the rain spattering against the window.

"Do you think you're the only person who worried about him? Who cared what became of him?" Mrs. Martin leaned across her desk toward me. "I had no choice, thanks to you, but to throw him out. Maybe the next time you want to help somebody, you'll remember Mr. Weems."

Wordlessly, I got to my feet and ran out of her office. How could it be my fault? Mr. Weems hadn't hurt me when he threw the magazine, anybody could see that.

Ignoring the people I bumped into, I rushed to the women's room and locked myself in a stall. I cried and cried, but Mrs. Martin's words wouldn't go away. Thanks to me, thanks to *me,* Mr. Weems had nowhere to go.

When I'd finally cried all the tears I had, I went back to the children's room, thinking I'd talk to Mrs. Hunter, but she was too busy helping kids to spare any time for me.

To escape from my thoughts, I picked up a well-read copy of the *Yellow Fairy Book.* While the rain fell and day darkened into night, I tried to lose myself in a story about a prince who rescues the Flower Queen's daughter from a dragon, but I kept hearing Mrs. Martin saying over and over again, "Thanks to you, thanks to you, thanks to you." In books like the one I was reading, there were happy endings, but in real life things just seemed to get worse and worse.

I don't know how much time passed before a voice suddenly broke into my thoughts.

"I've been looking all over the library for you. What are you doing in the children's room? I thought you were working on your report!"

I looked up at Dad and then I followed him glumly

out of the library into the rain. He started the car with a jerk and spun the tires leaving the parking lot. "Road's slippery," he muttered as we turned right on Warfield Parkway and started for home.

"What's this?" He slammed on the brakes and skidded to a stop at the end of two lanes of cars creeping forward at no more than five or ten miles an hour. Peering through the steamy windshield, he muttered, "There must have been an accident."

Terrific, I thought, just what I need — trapped in the car with the great attorney. Mrs. Martin had upset me so much already, I knew I'd start crying if Dad launched one of his attacks on my grades or my clothes or my attitude toward life in general. All I wanted to do was go home and retreat to my room and stay there for a couple of years.

"Damn," Dad muttered as he inched the car forward, then braked sharply. "Can you see which lane is blocked, Kelly?"

I rolled the window down and stuck my head out into the cold rain, but all I could see were taillights, steamed-up rear windows, and the blurred outlines of drivers and passengers.

Shaking my head, I closed the window, grateful for the warmth of the heater. "What do you think happened?" I asked, hoping to keep Dad's attention on the traffic jam. If we stayed in neutral territory, maybe he'd forget he was angry with me.

"Oh, some fool probably skidded into somebody else." Dad drummed his fingers on the steering wheel and sighed. "We're all being inconvenienced because a couple of idiots couldn't control their cars."

While Dad went on talking about the ineptitude of most drivers, I peered ahead. We were getting closer to the accident, and I could see flashing lights.

"It might be something more serious," I said. "There's an ambulance."

"They send ambulances nowadays for almost anything," Dad said. He leaned forward, but the rain made it hard to see. It was like looking through a wall of water.

Even if nobody was hurt, I didn't want to stare at the people I saw standing by the road. They were upset enough already, I thought, so I slid down in my seat, determined not to look, and glanced at Dad. In the red and blue flashes of light from a police car, I saw him frown and grip the steering wheel.

"Good God," he said, "it's that man, Kelly. Mr. Weems."

I sat up then, but Dad pushed me back down.

"No," he said, "Don't look."

But it was too late. I'd already seen the bags scattered on the road, ripped open, Mr. Weems's belongings spilling out on the asphalt. And something else, a body on a stretcher, a man covering it with a blanket, rolling it toward the waiting ambulance.

"Daddy!" I cried, "Stop, let me out!" I wanted to go to Mr. Weems, comfort him, collect his stuff. But Dad kept the car moving, increasing his speed as soon as we were past the red flares flickering in the rain.

I grabbed the door handle, thinking I'd jump out whether he stopped or not, but Dad's hand closed round my wrist, holding me tight.

"No, Kelly," he said. "It's too late, there's nothing you can do."

"What do you mean?" I yelled, but I knew, I knew, and there was a rock in my chest where my heart should have been.

Turning left so suddenly I bumped my head on the door, Dad pulled onto a side street. Coming to a stop, he did something he hadn't done for years. He put his arms around me and held me, pressing my face against his shoulder.

"He's dead, honey," he whispered.

"How do you know?" I jerked away, staring at him. "How can you tell?"

He shook his head. "I've seen dead bodies before, Kelly, lots of them." His voice shook. "And the way they covered him. I've seen that too many times." Then he put his head down on the steering wheel and sat there, as silent and motionless as a stone. "Oh, God," he whispered. "God."

Pressing my hands against my mouth, I watched the rain pour down. It ran in sheets across the street. It dripped from the bare tree limbs, it puddled on the sidewalk, and gleamed in the light shining from windows. And I listened to the noise it made, tapping on the roof, gurgling in the gutters, sluicing down the windshield.

Then we heard the sirens, the terrible wailing as the

ambulance sped past the end of the street, rushing along Warfield Parkway to the hospital. Where it would arrive too late.

"What will happen to him?" I whispered to Dad.

"They'll find his family, tell them. Then somebody will make the arrangements."

"Arrangements?" It was a word I'd known all my life but it had suddenly acquired a new meaning, and I couldn't think what it was. Something sinister and final, something scary.

"The funeral, the burial," Dad said, but if I hadn't seen his mouth moving I wouldn't have known it was his voice.

Yes, I thought, the coffin, the flowers, the grave — everything arranged just so. Sobbing, I leaned into him, my face pressing against his raincoat, and he held me again.

"It's the library's fault," I wept. "They kicked him out, told him he couldn't bring his bags inside anymore. That's why he was wandering around in the rain and the dark. He didn't have any place to go."

I cried harder, knowing it was my fault too. I'd just wanted to help him, and now this. If it hadn't been for me, Mr. Weems would be sitting in the reference room right this minute, reading his war books, safe and warm and dry. Why hadn't I left him alone?

Chapter 16

THE MINUTE DAD and I stepped into the kitchen, Mom knew something terrible had happened. She stood staring at us, her spoon poised over a steaming pot of spaghetti sauce. "What's wrong?" she whispered.

Without speaking, I hurled myself against her. While she held me tightly, I heard Dad trying to explain about Mr. Weems.

"It was awful," he said hoarsely. "The body on the stretcher, the cover over it, the rain, it was like Vietnam all over again."

"Oh, Greg," Mom whispered. Still circling me with one arm, she reached out to him. For a moment he let her hug him, then he pulled away.

"Sorry," he said, the old brusqueness suddenly returning to his voice. "This is ridiculous. I don't know what came over me. Getting all upset. I didn't even know the poor bastard."

He fumbled with his pipe, his hands shaking so hard he could barely strike the match. "Help your mother set the table, Kelly," he said abruptly and left Mom and me standing by the stove with Gandalf nosing round our feet.

As the door to the den closed behind him, I looked at Mom. "What's wrong with Dad?"

Mom poked the sauce with the spoon. "He just can't deal with Vietnam, what happened to him, what he saw, what he did." She stared past me at the closed door. "Things remind him sometimes, the smell of a dead possum by the side of the road, a helicopter overhead, a war movie. Now this."

As Mom turned away to dump noodles into the boiling water, I remembered the time Dad and I found a dead cat under the bushes in our front yard. It must have been hit by a car or something and crawled under there to die. It smelled awful, and flies were crawling on its eyes, and it was sort of flattened, like a stuffed animal a kid had left outside in the rain. He told me to get a plastic garbage bag, but when he tried to lift the cat on a shovel, he started throwing up.

I got scared and ran inside to get Mom. From the window, I watched her stroke Dad's hair and talk to him. Then she put the cat in the garbage bag, and later, she and I buried it in the backyard.

I'd been puzzled then. Seeing the cat had scared me; I'd never seen anything dead before, and the sight of it was pretty horrible, but Dad was a grownup. Why had it upset him more than me?

Now I knew, and I felt ashamed of myself for thinking Dad didn't have any feelings. During the fight we'd had before Thanksgiving, I'd accused him of being insensitive; I'd thought he'd forgotten all about the fighting and the dying, I'd thought he was somehow inferior to Mr. Weems.

But the war hadn't ended for Dad any more than it had for Mr. Weems. For both of them, Vietnam was still there, ready to leap out at them in the form of a hundred ordinary things.

"I feel so bad, Mom." My eyes filled with tears again as I leaned against her, fitting my head into the curve of her neck. "It's all my fault Mr. Weems is dead."

"What do you mean, Kelly?" Mom's arm tightened around me.

"The library kicked him out because of me. The night he threw the magazine, remember? They used that for an excuse."

"But, honey, he always walked in the road. It was dark and raining. The driver didn't see him."

I let her pat my back and hug me, but it didn't really comfort me. He'd told me to leave him alone, but I hadn't and now he was dead.

"No," I said, "I should have listened to him. He said he didn't want any help, but I kept on pestering him."

Mom drew back and stared at me. "You did the right thing, Kelly. Nobody else, myself included, did anything for Mr. Weems. We didn't even try. We just looked the other way and hoped someone else would do it."

She grabbed my shoulders and gave me a gentle shake. "At least you tried, honey. You cared." Then she hugged me again. "It's not your fault things didn't turn out the way you wanted them to."

"Do you really believe that?" I asked her. "Or are you just trying to make me feel better?"

"I'm ashamed of myself," Mom said, "for not trying to help Mr. Weems. But I'm proud of you."

*

When the three of us sat down at the dinner table, we didn't have much to say except, "Pass the bread" or "Can I have the margerine, please?" Every time I looked at Dad, he bent his head over his plate and busied himself eating; he obviously didn't want to talk about Mr. Weems or Vietnam or anything else. A stranger sharing a meal with us would have had more to say than he did.

Mom was quiet too. She didn't even shoo Gandalf when he leapt up on the table and stuck his nose into the margerine. I don't think she noticed him.

And me? I poked at my spaghetti, spending more time twirling it elaborately around my fork than actually eating it. I was sitting at the table because I didn't want to be alone, not because I was hungry.

"Kelly, stop playing with your food," Dad said suddenly, the first evidence of his old self.

Without looking at him, I picked up my plate and carried it to the kitchen with Gandalf at my heels.

"No, you're too fat already," I told him as I rinsed the plate. Before I went upstairs, I glanced into the dining room. Mom and Dad were sitting opposite each other, their faces softened by the little oil lamps burning in the center of the table. Neither was looking at the other. Neither was speaking. Dad was sipping wine, Mom was staring past him into the dark living room.

Grabbing my backpack full of books, I fled to my room, knowing I'd rather be truly alone than spend another minute watching my parents.

*

The next morning I saw Julie as I was heading toward my locker. To my surprise, she grabbed my sleeve as I started to walk past her.

"Did you hear about the bagman?" she asked. "He got killed on Warfield Parkway last night. He walked right in front of a car."

"I don't want to talk about it." Pulling away from her, I started twirling my lock.

"I thought you'd be really upset," Julie persisted.

Turning my back, I stuffed my jacket into my locker, fighting to keep from crying. Overnight I'd convinced myself Dad had been wrong. Mr. Weems hadn't been killed, just injured. He was safe in the hospital, and while he was there he'd get the help he needed, and the next time I saw him he'd be all clean and happy, working somewhere, living in a real house.

Now Julie was telling me what she'd heard from one of her neighbors, somebody who'd witnessed the whole thing. No use telling myself it wasn't true. Not anymore.

"Hey, Kelly," Keith's voice cut into Julie's, interrupting her. "I heard about Mr. Weems."

I looked up at him and the tears I'd been holding back came pouring down my cheeks. With Julie standing there, too surprised to say anything, Keith put his arms around me and let me cry.

Then the bell rang, and Julie said, "Come on, Keith, we'll be late for homeroom."

"Will you be all right, Kelly?" Keith held me at arm's length and stared down at me.

I rubbed my eyes and nodded. "Thanks," I said and then headed for my homeroom without looking back. I didn't want to watch him walk away with Julie.

I slid into my seat just before Miss Wisnewski got to my name in roll call. As the morning announcements droned from the intercom announcing bus delays, summoning students to the office, reminding us of club meetings and pep rallies, I heard Brett tell Doug he was going to look for Mr. Weems's bags.

"They must be scattered along Warfield Parkway," he said, but Doug was sure the police had picked up everything.

"He probably had drugs or booze or something in those bags," he said.

"Or money," Brett said. "Lots of old bums are loaded."

That was all they were interested in — what was in

Mr. Weems's bags. It was just like Shel Silverstein's poem. Nobody cared about his birthday, nobody cared where he'd been or where he was going or why he was blue. They only wanted to know what he had in his bags.

When the bell rang for first period, I trudged down the hall to French, too depressed to worry about the irregular verbs I hadn't learned. We were having a quiz, and I knew I'd flunk it. Worse yet, Courtney and Julie were in my class, and I was sure they'd be passing notes back and forth, glancing at me and giggling. Well, who cared?

Without looking in Julie's direction, I opened my French book to the section on irregular verbs. If I had a photographic memory I could pass the quiz.

To my surprise, a note folded a hundred times landed on my desk. I stared suspiciously at my name in Julie's handwriting. Then, while Miss Kennedy called roll, I opened it slowly.

Dear Kelly,
    I'm sorry about Mr. Weems — honest. I'll call you tonight — okay?
                            Julie
    P.S. Get a load of Lisa Hocker's jeans. How did she get them on I wonder !!!!!!!!

As Miss Kennedy passed out the quiz sheets, I glanced across the room at Julie and tried to smile at her, but I couldn't help wondering what we'd talk about tonight. Lisa Hocker's jeans maybe?

*

Sometime during the day, I decided what I was going to do for Mr. Weems. It was Mr. Hardy who gave me the idea. We'd finally finished reading the *Iliad,* and we were summarizing our feelings about war. As usual, the class got Mr. Hardy to digress, and he ended up telling us about the Vietnam memorial in Washington. I'd heard of it, of course, but I'd never seen it. While he was describing the black walls inscribed with the names of all the soldiers who had died in the war, it occurred to me that Mr. Weems's name should be there too. Hadn't he really died in Vietnam? Or at least because of Vietnam?

After class, I stopped to ask Mr. Hardy if you actually had to die in Vietnam to get your name on the wall.

"What do you mean, Kelly?"

"Well, suppose Vietnam really messed a person up, suppose his life was never the same afterward, like those soldiers in the World War One poems you read to us. And then the person died maybe twenty years later. Wouldn't he be a war casualty too? Just delayed?"

Mr. Hardy shook his head. "I see what you mean, but that's not how it works. You have to die on the battlefield or in a p.o.w. camp."

I must have looked disappointed because as I turned away, Mr. Hardy laid a hand on my shoulder. "Are you thinking about the man who was killed on the parkway last night?"

I nodded. "His name should be on that wall."

"If they added all the names of people like Mr. Weems," Mr. Hardy said, "they'd have to build another wall."

*

I walked home alone. It was the first of December, and the trees were bare. The wind rattled the branches over my head, and the sun, shining again after a week of rain, wasn't very warm. As I plodded along, I remembered what Mr. Hardy had told the class about the Vietnam memorial. People from all over the country visited it, and many of them brought things and laid them at the base of the wall. The last time he'd been there, he'd seen dog tags, flowers, photographs, letters, even a pair of old army shoes polished till they shone — possessions of the dead soldiers or tributes to them.

"What happens to all that stuff?" Brett had wanted to know.

"It's collected at the end of the day, tagged, and taken to a storehouse. Someday they plan to display it."

"None of it's thrown away?" Brett was amazed.

"It's all saved."

"Why?" Courtney asked.

"Well, it reveals a lot about the war, how we feel about it, how we're resolving it." Mr. Hardy's voice trailed off, and he looked relieved when Courtney asked a question about the test he was giving next week.

If everything left at the wall was saved, I knew what to do. I'd add Mr. Weems's name myself. It wouldn't be there permanently, not on the wall itself, but it would be taken away to the storehouse and saved with all the other things. It would show people the war wasn't over, not yet, not while people like Mr. Weems were still suffering and dying because of what happened to them in Vietnam.

Chapter 17

WHEN I GOT HOME, I took out my sketches of Mr. Weems. None of them was very good. No matter how hard I'd tried, I hadn't caught the true sadness of his face. It made me feel bad to look at all my muddled efforts and remember him sitting in the library, reading his books, trying hard not to bother anybody.

After a long time, I chose the one that came closest to a true likeness. I wrote Mr. Weems's name and the date he died. Then I added, "A casualty of the Vietnam War." In the remaining space, I copied a quote from one of the poems Mr. Hardy had given us, "December Stillness" by Siegfried Sassoon:

> *December stillness, crossed by twilight roads*
> *Teach me to travel far and bear my loads.*

Of all the poems, it seemed the most appropriate.

While I was in the kitchen putting the drawing into a clear plastic bag, Mom came up behind me.

"What are you doing?" she asked.

Since it was too late to hide the bag, I showed it to her. "I'm taking this to the Vietnam War memorial. I'm going to tape it on the wall."

Mom looked puzzled. "Someone will just take it away, honey," she said.

"I know, but they won't throw it out. They save everything that's left there, and someday it will all be on display in a museum. Then everybody will know about Mr. Weems. He'll be immortal."

Mom hugged me, but I pulled away. "It's not just a dumb little kid thing to do," I told her, imagining that was what she was thinking.

"Of course it isn't, Kelly. It's a wonderful idea."

"You won't tell Dad, will you?"

"Why don't you want him to know?"

"He'll think it's stupid." I pressed the edges of the bag together, sealing the picture inside.

Mom stroked my hair. "Why don't you ask your father to drive you down there. He's never seen the war memorial." She hesitated a minute. "It might do him good."

"I want you to take me," I muttered. "Not him."

"Ask him," she said. "Please?"

*

At dinner, I ate silently, glancing from time to time at my father. He seemed to have recovered from the shock of yesterday and was enjoying his food as usual.

Catching my eye at one point, he asked me about my report.

"I hope what happened to Mr. Weems won't make it too hard to write, Kelly," he said.

I swallowed hard and stared at him as he reached across the table and patted my hand. "Some things are difficult to understand when you're fourteen," he said. "But when you think about the kind of life he was living, how unhappy he was, maybe it's best for him not to struggle anymore."

"Julie said he stepped right in front of the car," I said. "He must have seen it coming. I know it was raining and dark, but the car had its lights on."

"You think he did it deliberately?" Mom asked.

"He might have," Dad said.

There was a little silence, and Mom glanced at me. I knew she wanted me to say something to Dad about going to the war memorial. Instead I took another piece of bread and busied myself buttering it.

Without looking at Dad, I said, "In a way, Mr. Weems is a casualty of the Vietnam War, just like the ones who have their names on that wall in Washington."

"Our troops left Vietnam in nineteen seventy-five, Kelly. You can't call a man who dies years later a war casualty."

"Vietnam killed him, Dad. Anybody could see that. It just took him a long time to actually die."

"Kelly has a point, Greg," Mom put in.

Dad leaned toward me. Was he about to go into the

great attorney routine and cross-examine me? "I've told you before thousands of men survived Vietnam, came home, and lived normal lives, myself and your Uncle Ralph among them."

"Yes, but you won't talk about it. You've never even been to the war memorial."

"What's the sense of digging up the past? The war's been over for me since nineteen seventy. Why should I talk about it or even think about it?"

"Because it's still eating away at you, Greg," Mom said quietly.

Dad looked at her and frowned. "A few nightmares and you think I need a psychiatrist," he said. "Next you'll be telling me to check into a V.A. hospital." The sarcasm he was aiming for failed, and he turned his attention to his food.

Mom sighed and gently shoved Gandalf off the table before he could grab the chicken bone on her plate. "Bad kitty," she said without much conviction as he retreated to the kitchen and sniffed his empty dish.

"You spoil that cat," Dad said, then turned back to me. "Don't get me wrong," he said. "I'm sorry as hell for that poor guy, Kelly, but sometimes I think you'd appreciate me more if I packed all my belongings in a couple of garbage bags and started wandering around Adelphia in rags."

"Your belongings wouldn't fit in a couple of bags," I pointed out. "You'd have to get a U-Haul just for your electronic stuff."

"Oh, give me a break, Kelly." Dad took the coffee

pot from Mom and poured himself a cup. "Since when is it a crime to earn a good living?"

I frowned at the steam rising from my coffee. How could I answer his question? No matter what I said, Dad would just dismiss me as a kid who didn't know anything about life. But it seemed to me he was evading the real issue. If you spend all your time and energy making money, aren't you neglecting a lot of other important stuff? Isn't it kind of selfish?

Take Courtney, for instance. She really admires my father because he's a big success. In fact, she wants to go to law school so she can make a lot of money, just like Dad. That's how she defines success — getting rich.

But to me, that's not success. Georgia O'Keeffe and Ansel Adams, or Keith's hero, Farley Mowat — I want to be like them. Artists and photographers and writers who make other people care about important things like beauty and conservation and animals.

Or if I can't be an artist, if I'm not talented enough, then maybe I can be like Aunt Eliza. She isn't famous or rich, but she's the most successful person I know.

*

After dinner, Dad disappeared into the den to work on a case, and I followed Mom upstairs to her studio. "If you won't take me to Washington, can I ask Aunt Eliza?" I asked her.

"You heard what I said about your father." Mom flipped on her tape deck, and Joan Baez's voice eddied around the room, high and sweet, in a sad song about a selkie and his son. I watched Mom dip a tiny brush into a jar of scarlet ink and begin painting the cape of a prince on an ebony horse galloping across a snowy field. All along the horizon behind him, she'd inked in a dark forest, and the prince was looking back as if he were afraid of something he'd seen in the trees.

"But you heard Dad at dinner," I said. "You know he won't take me."

"You haven't asked him yet. You don't know what he'll say," Mom said without looking at me.

"Aunt Eliza would love to go."

"Kelly, don't disappoint me. Please ask your father." She looked at me, her face stern, the prince momentarily forgotten.

Glumly I went back downstairs and knocked on Dad's door. When he told me to come in, I approached him slowly. "What is it?" he asked, frowning at me over a pile of papers on his desk.

"You know the war memorial in Washington?"

"Yes. What about it?"

"Well, I need to go there."

"Has it got something to do with your report?"

I nodded. "I want to describe it, but I've never seen it, so I was wondering if maybe on Saturday or Sunday you could drive me down there."

"From what I've read, there's not much to see," Dad said. "It's just a hole in the ground."

"I really need to go. If you can't take me, maybe Aunt Eliza could."

"No, no, don't bother your aunt with a request like

166 ·

that. It would be a hell of a long drive for her." He sighed and rearranged his papers. "I'll take you."

"Saturday?"

He nodded and lit his pipe. "Ten o'clock."

I paused a moment, hesitating. When he looked up at me, I bent toward him and gave him a fast kiss on the cheek. "Thanks, Dad."

He put an arm around my waist and gave me a quick hug. "It's no big deal," he said.

We looked at each other silently, sizing each other up like strangers meeting for the first time. Then Dad grinned. "Go on," he said. "I've got work to do."

A few days ago, a dismissal like that would have made me mad, but tonight I could see he was sort of joking and sort of serious. He wasn't angry at me, he wasn't tired of me, he just wanted time to work.

I ran upstairs to my room, but on the way, I stopped in the doorway of Mom's studio. "He's taking me," I told her.

She looked up from her painting and smiled. "I'm really pleased, Kelly."

I ran to her side and kissed her good night, glad I'd made her happy. Then, while Gandalf dozed beside me on a pile of drawings, I started my paper for Mr. Poland. As I worked in quotes from Wilfred Owen and Siegfried Sassoon, I realized I was actually enjoying a homework assignment. For the first time I felt I was doing something important, something that really mattered, not just performing a dull task to pass a class.

Chapter 18

SATURDAY WAS COLD and gray, overcast but with no real sign of rain. No wind either, just a damp December chill penetrating your clothes and making your toes and fingers ache.

To keep warm, I pulled on a pair of long johns and searched under my bed for my only pair of jeans without holes. Then I put on a sweater Dad had given me for Christmas last year; it was kelly green, the color of my eyes Dad said, and even though it wasn't as baggy as my favorite sweaters, it looked okay.

I found Dad in the kitchen reading the stock market news and drinking coffee. Although he glanced at my granny boots and rhinestone earrings, he watched me fix myself my usual raisin bread and jam sandwich without saying a word.

"Do you think Mr. Weems will have a funeral?" I'd read the obituary page of the *Washington Post* every day since the accident, but I hadn't seen Mr. Weems's name yet.

Dad took a sip of coffee. "Probably not, Kelly," he said. "It would have been in the paper by now."

"But they haven't even put his name in. I thought everybody who died got his name in the paper."

Dad shook his head. "Only if somebody sends it in."

That didn't seem right. When you died, shouldn't you get a little attention? Otherwise you just disappeared like a raindrop in the ocean. "I wanted to go to his funeral," I told Dad.

"I imagine it was private," Dad said.

There was a silence then, and I could hear one of Mom's albums, Simon and Garfunkel again, singing "Parsley, Sage, Rosemary and Thyme." Gandalf rubbed against my legs and purred, hoping I'd drop some food his way, and the old clock in the living room chimed the half hour.

"It's nine-thirty," Dad said. "Why don't we go?"

*

Dad was pretty quiet as we headed down the interstate toward Washington. He was the sort of person who said he couldn't drive and talk at the same time, so he let me listen to the radio as long as I didn't switch stations or turn it up too loud. That meant I was at the mercy of a disk jockey named Weasel who played pretty decent music. This morning he was doing groups like Sibling Rivalry and Final Conflict, the kind of cynical, satirical stuff I like.

By the time we were driving along Constitution

Avenue, looking for a place to park, Dad seemed a little tense. "Do you have to listen to that crap?" he asked as Splintered Glass was finishing up a song about nuclear war.

"What's wrong with it?"

"What's right with it? You can't dance to it, let alone sing along with it. No melody. You can't even understand most of the words."

I took a deep breath and looked Dad right in the eye. "I bet your parents didn't think much of the Grateful Dead," I said. "They probably thought you should be listening to Frank Sinatra or some big band with a great beat."

"What are you talking about?" Dad turned his head away, scanning the street for a parking place.

"Mom says you were a real Dead Head when you came back from Vietnam," I told him.

"For God's sake, Kelly," Dad said, "that was years ago."

"Well, all I'm saying is you had your music, and I have mine."

"Yes, but the Dead had something to say." Dad slowed down, his eyes on a blue Toyota backing out of a parking place just ahead.

I rolled my eyes. Everybody knew what the Dead had to say. "So does Splintered Glass," I said.

Dad began maneuvering his car into the empty space left by the Toyota. "There was a lot more to the Dead than some people think," he muttered.

"Next you'll be telling me 'what a long, strange trip

it's been.'" In case he needed reminding, I started humming the chorus.

Dad looked at me and actually smiled. "Well," he said, "as a matter of fact, it has been a long strange trip, Kelly. Just wait till you're my age. You'll know what I mean then."

Locking the car door, Dad started walking down Constitution Avenue. "It's about three blocks straight ahead," he said. As he spoke, his breath puffed out like smoke in the cold, still air, and I could almost imagine the words appearing in them like comic-strip balloons.

Shoving my hands in the pockets of my army jacket, I walked along behind Dad, trying to picture him listening to the Grateful Dead in the apartment Mom had described, but I finally had to give up. I'd seen photographs of Dead Heads in beads and tie-dyed T-shirts and faded jeans, long hair held back with headbands. No way could Dad have ever worn outfits like that! His idea of scruffy was a pair of corduroy slacks and a button-down shirt without a tie.

After a while, I looked up and saw he was way ahead of me, burning up the sidewalk as if he were racing everybody in sight. Nothing unusual in that. Or in the fact he was winning. Sometimes I can't imagine Dad sleeping — he just doesn't relax long enough. Every second of every day he's out there competing with the rest of the world.

Me, though — most of the time I poke along, dragging my feet, not especially eager to get where I'm going. Today was definitely a slow day for me. In fact, the closer I got to the war memorial, the less sure I was that I wanted to see it. I was beginning to feel the way I had when our seventh-grade class went on a field trip to Antietam, a Civil War battlefield way out in the Maryland countryside.

It was a spring day, as I remember, soft and green and warm, and the boys were running around, talking about battle tactics, and the girls were taking pictures of each other sitting on the cannons, and I was staring at a little stone house across the road, thinking how peaceful it all seemed.

Then I happened to glance at a display of photographs mounted on stands near me. The camera must have been set up behind me. In the pictures, you could see the little stone house and the cannons, but instead of a bunch of kids laughing and shouting and pretending to shoot each other, there were dead soldiers sprawled on the ground. What I was looking at — the stone house, the green fields, the blue sky full of creamy clouds — was the last thing those men ever saw.

I jumped back and my eyes filled up with tears and I could hardly breathe, but everybody else was still laughing and running around. They acted as if the war had happened so long ago it didn't matter anymore. In fact, some of the boys lay down and pretended to be dead while their friends took their pictures.

Even though my teacher was mad, I went back to the school bus and sat there all by myself till it was time to go home; nobody was going to make me put one foot on that battlefield.

Now I knew the soldiers whose names were on the wall of the Vietnam memorial hadn't died in Washington, D.C., and I knew their bodies weren't buried there. But I felt as if I were going to a funeral home or a graveyard, a huge one like Arlington National Cemetery where the white stone markers stretch out in rows all the way to the horizon.

As I hesitated, I realized Dad had stopped too. He was squinting at a little park service sign pointing the way to the memorial. Even though there wasn't anything to read except a few words, we both stared at the sign as if it concealed a hidden message, something we had to decode.

Over our heads, the pale gray sky seemed enormous, its still expanse stabbed by the Washington Monument poking up from a grassy hill on the Mall. Seagulls circled above us, crying, while others perched on streetlights watching us. At our feet, pigeons strutted back and forth, bobbing their heads like wind-up toys looking for food.

"It's this way," Dad said suddenly, as if he'd just figured out what the arrow on the sign meant. He started slowly down the path, content to let a group of camera-laden tourists pass him, and I followed.

Chapter 19

AHEAD OF US, I saw people walking solemnly down a ramp into the ground, a long parade of them, all moving quietly, pausing sometimes before they disappeared. A little farther away, Abraham Lincoln sat on his big stone chair, watching them from between the pillars of his memorial. His face was long and sad.

As I walked closer, I realized the war memorial wasn't as deep as I'd imagined it would be. Two black walls cut into the ground; where they met, they were about ten feet tall, but at the ends they tapered off to a few inches. When you walked into it, it was like the war itself; you sank in step by step, and all of a sudden you were in over your head.

Dad paused to examine what appeared to be a telephone book on a pedestal. "Go on ahead if you want to," he said. "I'll catch up later."

"What are you looking at?" I peered over his shoulder, wanting to delay my confrontation with the wall.

"This is how you find the names." He pointed to the page. "See? It gives the location of each one."

"How many names are there?" I stared at the thickness of the book.

"Fifty-eight thousand, one hundred and fifty-six," said a little boy. "On the wall, they list who died each day the war was fought." He paused to tap a brochure with his finger. "They do it that way because they're 'showing the war as a series of individual human sacrifices and giving each name a special place in history.'" He read slowly and carefully, stumbling a little over the words.

Dad and I stared at him. He was about eleven, I guess, and very serious.

"My uncle was killed in Vietnam," he explained. Then he held up a small piece of paper with a pencil rubbing on it. Roger Dietz, it said. "I made this. If you can't reach your relative's name, you can ask that man with the ladder. He'll do it for you."

I looked where the boy was pointing. Sure enough, a man was standing on a ladder near the place the walls joined, making a rubbing for a group of people watching him. Like me, he was wearing an army jacket.

As I walked down into the memorial with the little boy at my side, I looked back at Dad. "Are you coming?"

"In a little while." He was bent over the directory, taking notes on a piece of paper.

"My name's Roger," the boy said, "after my uncle. My dad's brother."

"I'm Kelly." I was staring at the names carved on the shiny black walls. I could see my reflection and Roger's, as well as other people's. Behind us all was the sky and the clouds. A few names had flowers taped next to them, one had a piece of paper that said, "I love you," and another had a cross. Dog tags leaned against the base of the wall, along with more flowers and crosses and photographs of young guys in army uniforms.

Looking at all those things made me feel like crying, so I bit my lip hard and blinked my eyes and gazed at the Washington Monument instead. It seemed to me then that everything around me had something to do with war. The American Revolution, the Civil War, Vietnam. In other places, you could find World War I and World War II memorials, not to mention Korea and other wars I didn't know much about. History was nothing but a series of wars and men dying.

When the Third World War blew us all to atoms, who would be left to design the memorial?

Roger nudged me then. "Who died in your family?" he asked.

"Nobody." I wanted him to go away, not to be here while I picked the place to leave Mr. Weems's memorial.

"Why are you here then?"

"Just to see it." I was reading names to myself. George W. Ellis, Alton J. Fennel, Richard W. Fischer,

Ronald L. Fox, Roger C. Foxworth — on and on. Who were they? Where had they come from? What would they be doing now if they hadn't gone to Vietnam?

"Here's my uncle." Roger stopped and pointed to the name. "Twenty-eight E, Eighty-one. Right there." His fingers moved over the letters, tracing each one gently, reverently. "He died in nineteen sixty-seven."

"How old was he?" I touched the letters too, seeing my finger's reflection as it moved slowly across Roger Dietz's name.

"Nineteen," Roger said. "He was going to be an architect, but he couldn't afford college unless he got the G.I. Bill, so he joined the army and they sent him to Vietnam."

"Do you remember him?"

"Heck, no. He died before I was born, but my daddy talks about him a lot." Roger looked around. "I better get going. My mom's probably looking everywhere for me."

I watched Roger run back up the ramp and join a group in front of a statue of three soldiers. The statues were staring straight at the memorial and their faces were sad and full of fear and confusion as if they were the ghosts of all the names, still wondering why they had to die.

I saw Dad too, his back to me, standing in front of the statue. Was he ever coming down here, I wondered.

I walked past the man on the ladder as he climbed down and handed a rubbing to an old lady. She put the piece of paper into her wallet as if it were the most valuable thing she owned.

After I'd walked up and down a couple of times, and Dad still hadn't joined me, the man with the ladder asked me if he could help me find a name.

"I'm just waiting for my dad," I told him.

"Where is he?"

"Up there by those statues. He keeps saying he's coming, but then he doesn't."

"He's a veteran, isn't he?" The man had a kind face, big and coarse-featured, and he wore a name tag that said he was Paul Novak, a volunteer.

I nodded. "He never talks about it though."

"I'm a vet myself," Mr. Novak said, "and I can tell you it was hard for me to tell anyone about what I saw, what I did, what I felt. It was hard for me to come here the first time, real hard."

"He's never been here," I said.

Mr. Novak nodded. "Vets have a lot of trouble the first time. They hesitate a lot. Take a step toward it, then two steps back."

I looked at Dad. Sure enough, he was wandering around, pausing again to look at the directory.

"Maybe I should talk to him," Mr. Novak said. "It's not easy to see the names of your buddies on the wall. It stirs up a lot of guilt. You ask yourself how come you're alive and they're not."

He shoved his hands in his pockets and rocked back

and forth on his heels. "One reason I spend so much time volunteering is to help vets like your dad. You'd be surprised how many guys have never really gotten over the war. They put up a good front, some of them, but it still gives them nightmares."

As Dad started toward us, Mr. Novak went to meet him. I thought Dad would ignore him, but I was wrong. He stood there in his corduroy trousers and his tweed sports jacket and let this stranger in old army clothes take his arm and talk to him.

While I waited, shifting back and forth from foot to foot to keep warm, I realized nobody was near me. Quickly I knelt at the intersection of the walls and leaned my little bag against the east wall. I could see my reflection, but no one else's as I taped it in place. Hoping nobody had noticed what I'd done, I stood up and backed away, taking one last look at the sad face I'd drawn.

"They'll know now, Mr. Weems," I told him. "They'll know what happened to you, how long it took you to die from what they did to you."

My eyes filled with tears as I thought of him sitting in the library all by himself week after week. Had he learned anything at all from those books?

"I'm sorry, Mr. Weems," I whispered as the wind tugged at the clear bag and rippled his face. "I wish I could have helped you."

Overhead, a seagull cried, and I remembered the evening Mr. Weems and I fed the ducks together. He'd talked to me then; for half an hour, he'd trusted me.

But that was all. I sighed, letting my breath out slowly in a smoky cloud. Then I turned back toward Dad.

He and Mr. Novak were standing side by side, and Dad was tracing names with his fingers. "Jeff Adler, Nathan Braun, Joseph Peterson," he whispered. Then his hand dropped to his side and he stood still, staring at the wall.

"They were in your platoon?" Mr. Novak asked and Dad nodded.

"It happened a month before we were supposed to go home," Dad said. "They were just blown to hell with a mine. I had to help get them out of there. What was left of them."

Tears ran down Dad's face, and Mr. Novak put an arm around his shoulders. "I know how you feel," he said.

Dad shook his head. "I was twenty years old and all I could think was 'Thank God, it wasn't me.' I was wounded, see. Not too badly, but bad enough to go home, and I was so glad to be getting out of there alive. They were dead, not me, and I was glad. Glad — what kind of a man is glad at a time like that?"

Mr. Novak patted Dad's back. "A normal man," he said.

I took Dad's arm. "I'm glad too," I whispered, pressing my face against the rough wool of his sleeve.

He held me for a minute, pressing me against him, shutting out the gray sky and the black wall and all the names. "Let's go home, Kelly," he said.

He touched the three names again, then shook Mr. Novak's hand. "Thanks," he said.

Mr. Novak smiled and cuffed Dad's arm lightly. "It's what I'm here for," he said.

Dad nodded. "Are you ready, Kelly?"

As we walked slowly up the ramp, Dad paused to stare at Mr. Weems's picture. "Did you put this here, Kelly?" He knelt down to see it better.

Uncomfortably I edged away from him. "I had to," I whispered, "I just had to. You aren't going to make me take it down are you? Because I won't!"

Dad straightened up. A slight breeze lifted his hair, then dropped it. He bent his head for a moment and wiped his eyes with the back of his hand. "I'm glad you put it there, Kelly," he said. "It was the right thing to do."

I stared at him, hardly believing what I was hearing. It was the first time in a long, long while that Dad had told me I'd done something right.

The breeze quickened, and Mr. Weems's picture fluttered. Dad knelt again and pressed the tape more firmly against the wall. Then he put his arm around my shoulders, and we walked slowly away from the memorial, leaving the names behind, 58,156 plus one.